Noel's Hart

The Snowberry Series Book 3

Katie Mettner

ISBN-10 : 1505304113
ISBN-13 : 978-1505304114

Cover design by: Carrie Butler
Printed in the United States of America

Chapter One

I walked through the building, my eyes darting around the dark dining room of the old eatery. Buck's Tackle Barn was, in fact, not a barn, and it didn't sell tackle. It was an outdated restaurant with small, dingy, outdated octagon windows overlooking the street. Under my feet was a grungy carpet that had seen better days a decade ago. There were mismatched tables, covered in tablecloths decorated with 80's style red globed candles, to finish the look.

I stood with my hand on my hip and surveyed the room. I would love to say it was homey or even that it had charm, but all I could say was it needed a good scrub down and massive updating before anyone could even think about making it a profitable business again.

I steeled my shoulders and walked toward the kitchen. After seeing the condition of the dining room, I was afraid of what I would find.

The swinging doors were barely closed behind me when I stumbled backward into them. The kitchen literally glowed from the massive amount of stainless steel surrounding me. It was state of the art, top of the line, and spotless.

I rubbed my chin thoughtfully. Maybe I judged Buck's a little prematurely. The door to the walk-in cooler was slightly ajar and I stuck my head in, expecting to recoil from the smell of rotten meat or spoiled vegetables. Instead, I was pleasantly surprised to find it was brand new, never used, and up to code with safety features.

"As you can see, the whole kitchen has been redone." The real estate agent, Jerry, pointed out as he leaned against the stove. "Buck barely had it finished before he suffered the stroke. He never even turned that cooler on." He pointed to the dark cavern where I stood. "His next project was the dining room, which does need some updating."

"I'm sorry, Jerry. I can tell Buck was a big part of this community. It's a shame he won't be able to come back to work."

He nodded, and I wandered back to the dining room. "With the kitchen being completely overhauled already, it puts a whole different spin on this project, in my opinion. The dining area needs some work to make it a true Kiss's Cafe, but I can see the potential." I was in the middle of the dining area again, my mind's eye removing all of the tables and carpet, inserting a counter, hardwood floors, and a cut-out window for the cook.

Jerry cleared his throat behind me. "Buck and his wife are willing to make a deal with the right person. They have no children, and their only niece isn't interested in the business. If you'd like,

I could take you over there so you can talk with them. Buck can't get around too well yet, but he's still got all his marbles."

I walked around the dining room again, picturing booths along the outside walls, and a long counter the length of the room. "This building would require a different set-up than what I usually have, but perhaps it's time for a change. Buck's Tackle Barn might be that change," I pondered aloud.

Jerry shifted nervously and finally sat down in one of the rickety wooden chairs. "This town needs a family restaurant. I'm afraid we'll lose residents if we don't have a place for them on Friday night for their fish fry and Saturday morning pancakes," Jerry lamented, nervously wringing his hands.

I shook off my musings and picked up the info sheet he had hastily put together. The building wasn't on the market yet, and Jerry was just doing Buck a favor by showing me the place.

"Family-style dining is my specialty, Jerry. All my cafés are set up as a family dining experience for large groups, or dinner service for smaller groups. Dining in Kiss's Café is all about what the customer wants. What's the need in Snowberry for twenty-four-hour service? Would it be necessary?" I asked, trying to get a feel for a town which I had only begun to know.

"Twenty-four-hour service, you say? Nah, not in Snowberry. If you open when the sun comes up and close when it goes down, you'll be fine around these parts. No one here is open twenty-four hours other than the hospital and the morgue." He laughed heartily at his own joke, and I had to bite back a smile.

"Jerry, do you think we can drop in on Buck and his wife this morning?" I asked, checking my watch.

He clapped his hands once and nodded eagerly. "Jump in my truck and I'll take you over."

December

"December!" a voice called. I turned quickly, surprised to see my twin brother jogging toward me. "Deccy, I need to talk to you," he huffed, stopping in front of me.

"I didn't think I would see you until the reception Saturday night. Is something wrong, Noel?" I asked, concerned.

"Sorry, I didn't mean to scare you. Is there somewhere we can talk?" He glanced around the hospital corridor.

"You betcha. I was just going down to the cafeteria for some lunch. Want to join me?"

He nodded solemnly and followed me down the set of stairs that opened into a large dining room. I grabbed a tray and handed him one, picking up a sandwich and fruit while I tried to get a read on why he was here.

"How's Jay?" he asked, grabbing a piece of chocolate cake from the cooler.

"He's great. We're very happy." I was gushing. I knew it, but I couldn't help it. Ever since I married Jay on Christmas Eve, it happened whenever someone mentioned his name. I pointed at his tray. "I see you still have a soft spot for sweets." I grinned, and he nodded sheepishly.

"Hey, a guy can't live on meat alone." He winked, and I smiled at the memories that line brought back.

We picked a table in the far back and set our trays down simultaneously, something that used to happen a lot back in the day. He motioned for me to go first. I sat, cracking open my Diet Coke and waiting for him to talk to me. When he didn't, I prodded him along.

"What brings you to Snowberry, brother? We aren't exactly on the way to anywhere," I pointed out, and he grimaced with his fork halfway to his mouth.

"No, I'm here for a reason," he admitted, setting the fork down. "I need a change, Deccy."

I leaned forward over the table and raised a brow. "What does that mean, Noel? You've always been the levelheaded one."

He smiled, and it went all the way to his eyes. He picked up my hand and held it. "What I mean is, my heart needs a change. Nick has worked hard, and that restaurant should have been his years ago, I just haven't had a reason to move on."

"I see," I responded slowly. The café in Rochester had been in the family forever, and I wasn't sure about it going to a new family. Granted, Nick had been a friend since we were in high school, and obviously has the work ethic to keep it up and running, but it was where I grew up. "Did you come to ask my permission to finally make Nick the owner-operator of the café in Rochester? You don't have to. I don't own stock in the business anymore," I reminded him, trying to keep the hurt out of my voice.

He fidgeted in his chair a little and let go of my hand. "That's not entirely true."

"Noel, you bought me out, remember? I don't have a legal right to any of it."

"I bought out your half of the franchise name, but the deed for that specific café is in both our names. The only way I can sell it, or hand it over to someone else, is if we both agree. We would both have to sign on the dotted line," he informed me.

"I don't understand why. I also don't understand why you never told me that," I admitted, a little more hurt creeping into my tone.

"I didn't know for a long time, to be honest. That café was the first one Mom and Dad ever owned, so it was left to the both of us. I thought after I bought you out, that would be the end of it, but my lawyer told me a few years ago if I wanted to transfer the deed to a new owner, I needed you to sign."

I waved my hand. "Wait, if you've known for years, why didn't you just have him draw up papers and send them to me? I would have signed them."

He shrugged and didn't meet my eyes. "I know you would have, and I don't have a good reason to offer other than if I didn't have the legal right to get rid of the building, then I would just have to stay."

I took a drink of my soda and looked him in the eye. What I saw there told me more than the words coming from his mouth.

"Because Rochester is safe and comfortable, so as long as the business needed you, it was a good reason to stay in your comfort zone?"

He nodded. "Exactly. I mean, I've started new cafes, but I always knew I had my home, and that café, to come back to. There was no risk, and I always had a soft landing place when I turned the key over to the new owner. If I give this one to Nick, then all of a sudden, things aren't so easy. I will have to step outside my comfort zone, big time."

"If you don't want to hand over the family building, Noel, just open a new café and give Nick control of the new one. That way, you can keep the original café and continue to use it as a training restaurant for your franchise," I reasoned.

My brother's business plan involved working with a new owner-operator, training them to run the café, and then handing them off the deed and franchise license once they had made enough excess revenue to make a down payment. It was a genius plan, and he now had seven cafes in Minnesota.

"I could do that, but that's not going to give me the kind of change I need, not personally anyway. I'm tired, Deccy. I've been doing twenty-four hours a day for my whole life, it seems. I'm not getting any younger and seeing you with Jay, well." He tossed up his hand a little before he took a bite of his cake, his eyes averted.

"Noel, I want you to be happy, that's all I've ever wanted. I prayed for the last eight years that you were happy. If you want to get out of the restaurant business, I'm not going to discourage you."

He glanced up and shook his head. "No, no, you misunderstood. I love what I do, but I want to do less of it, and in a different place."

"Oh, so you want to give Nick the old building and then start a restaurant somewhere else?" I asked, trying to get a feel for his plan.

He tapped his nose. "Bingo."

"It would be a nice change for you. Get out of Rochester and find a new town to invest your time and energy in. Do you have any prospects?" I asked, the food sitting in my belly like a lead balloon. We only just started mending our relationship, and if he moved away, I might never get to be part of his life again. I steeled my shoulders and made myself the promise that no matter where he went, I would make an effort to see him. I couldn't live like I had for the last eight years when I didn't have my twin by my side.

"I bought a place today, actually." He smiled, and my fork clattered to my plate. My hand was shaking terribly, and I hid it under the table.

"What? That was fast. Is it far away? What kind of restaurant is it? I guess you're serious about this. Is the town nice?" I couldn't stop asking questions, and he leaned forward and took hold of my shoulder.

"Slow down. Let me answer one at a time." He leaned back in his chair then and stuck his leg out. "I'll answer the last first. It's a small town, but lovely, and they don't have a family diner. The realtor assured me the town desperately needs one, and would wholeheartedly support one. He also told me the sidewalks roll up about nine at night, so staying open twenty-four hours wouldn't be necessary."

"That sounds like Snowberry. I always joke with Jay about how much I love that they roll up the sidewalk at nine every night, and don't open until the sun comes up every morning."

"I'm going to love having some time when the restaurant is closed. I can enjoy the town square at night and everything the town has to offer. There's a beautiful lake for summertime swimming and fishing, and rumor has it, the best hospital outside of Mayo Clinic." He nodded, folding his arms over his chest.

I thought back to the first time I went to Snowberry Lake with Jay. The snow hadn't fallen yet, but it was beautiful even in the late fall, with the berries heavy on the trees and the stars in the sky.

"The place sounds quaint and relaxing. What's the town's name? Have I been there?" I asked, trying to be happy for him, even if it meant we wouldn't see each other as much.

"Snowberry," he whispered, blowing me a kiss.

My mind raced to catch up. "Wait, you bought a restaurant in Snowberry?"

I leaned forward, and so did he, checking around for eavesdroppers. "The paperwork has to be finished yet, but today I made a deal with Buck and his wife to buy Buck's Tackle Barn. I'll be reopening it as a Kiss's Café."

My hand went to my mouth and started to shake. "Noel, I don't even know what to say."

He looked a little crestfallen but finally took my hand. "Say you're happy for me and excited I'll be living here?"

I jumped up and threw my arms around his neck, "Of course, I'm happy for you and excited! A few months ago, we weren't even talking, and now this. Forgive me, I'm in shock."

He hugged me tightly around my waist and chuckled a little. "I'm in a little bit of shock myself, but I'm delighted. It will take a little time to get the café redone and open, but I'll use that time to get settled and meet my neighbors."

I scooted back to my chair but was too excited to eat my food. My twin brother was moving to Snowberry, and would finally be part of my life. “You’re going to live in Snowberry,” I sighed. “You’re going to get to see Snow and Dully’s family grow, and hopefully mine and Jay’s.” His smile grew, and that’s when I remembered exactly where Buck's Tackle Barn was. Christmas Eve and Christmas Day played through my mind, and suddenly, the whole picture was revealed. "Noel, you've already met your neighbor. Savannah's Flower Emporium is right next door to Buck's."

He answered me with nothing more than a wink.

Chapter Two

Noel

I sat in my truck a few blocks down from Buck's, or rather my restaurant. I hadn't been able to wipe the smile off my face since I told December I was moving to Snowberry. I didn't expect her to cry, but she did, which told me even though I hadn't been the best brother lately, she still loved me. I promised I would be back on Saturday for their wedding reception and asked her not to tell anyone but Jay about my plans. It wouldn't take long for word to get around once the ink was dry, but until then, I had a few other people to tell first.

I hung up the phone from the realtor who was calling to tell me the papers were already prepped. I agreed to meet him at Buck's house tomorrow to sign them and take ownership of the building. I'd never had a deal move so quickly, but Buck and his wife were struggling to pay his bills, so I imagine they were happy to relinquish it to the first interested party. The fact that everything had come together so quickly also told me I was doing the right thing. This was meant to be. I needed to find myself and to do that, I had to quit hiding behind my parents' legacy.

I snorted at myself. *As if opening six other cafés was hiding behind your parent's legacy, Noel. Just give it up and admit the real reason you're here.*

My eyes locked on the building next to mine, and I rubbed my hands on my pants. She may have seen my truck earlier and wondered why I didn't stop in. She was first on that list of people I wanted to tell myself. I straightened my tie and picked up the to-go cup of coffee I grabbed for her on the way over. You can't really bring flowers to a florist, so I hoped coffee was the better choice to get my foot in the door.

I climbed out of the truck and locked the door. *Deep breath, Noel. She doesn't bite.* I straightened my suit jacket and strode across the street. If there was one thing I hated, it was a suit. My skinny, string bean physique always made me look like I was drowning in pinstripes. I was more of jeans and a flannel shirt kind of guy.

I paused in front of Savannah's Flower Emporium and took another deep breath. I hadn't seen her since Christmas Day, but I had sent her a few texts to check on her. She always assured me she was fine, but I knew she wasn't. It only took one look at her face to see she was far from fine.

I pulled the door open, and the scent of fresh roses, carnations, and violets hit me square in the face. I inhaled the scent of the fragrant petals, surprised by how it made you feel like it was spring in the middle of a cold, harsh winter. I made a mental note to have fresh flowers at the café year-round. I grinned. I bet my neighbor could supply them for me, too.

The door closed behind me, but I didn't see Savannah in the front room. I waited by the counter for a few moments, but when she didn't appear, I walked toward the backroom. From what she told me at Christmas, that's where she cuts and sorts flowers and does paperwork.

"Savannah? Are you here?" I called, so I didn't scare her if she just hadn't heard the bell. I peeked through the open door, and she had her back to me, wiping her face. "Savannah, are you okay?"

She nodded, wiping her hands on her apron. "Hi, Noel. I wasn't expecting you today."

My eyes drifted to the desk where there was paperwork spread out. Her computer screen was black, but the CPU still hummed. She still hadn't turned to make eye contact, so I walked in and put my hand on her shoulder until she did.

I took in the sight before me and sighed. Her cheeks were red, her eyes still harbored a few unshed tears, and the right side of her face was pulled back in a strange grimace.

"Do you need help?" I asked quickly, worried she might collapse again like Christmas Eve.

She shook her head and took a shaky breath. "No," her hand went to the side of her face to cover it, "everything is fine. I didn't hear the bell. It's nice to see you. What are you doing here?"

She ducked her head and tried to scoot around

me, but I stepped to the side, too. "Take a minute and get yourself together, honey. There's no one out there." She nodded her head quickly but kept her gaze on the floor. "I brought you some coffee," I told her, holding the cup out. She took it and whispered, *thank you.*

Either she was lying to me about her face or something terrible had just happened because I could hear the tears in her voice. I knelt down on the floor, gazing up at her under her long auburn hair. "Is it just one of those days where you could use a hug?"

"I suppose it would be if I had someone to hug," she said sadly.

I stood and took the cup from her hand, tugging her over into my arms. "You can hug me," I assured her, smiling when her arms slipped around my waist. At just a hair over five feet tall, her head barely reached the middle of my chest, but she rested it there like I was made for her. "I'm sorry you're having a hard day. Is there anything I can do?"

She sighed and shook her head, so I tucked her hair behind her ear and tried to comfort her the only way I knew how.

"Whatever it is, it will be okay. Maybe not today or tomorrow, but it will be," I promised. As we stood together in the silence of the room, I had never felt more intimate with another person.

She leaned back and tried to smile, but only the left side of her face moved. "I'm not so sure about that. Thanks for the hug," she picked up the cup, "and the coffee. You never did tell me what brought you to Snowberry."

I raised a brow and rocked back on my heels. Okay, she doesn't want to talk about it. I would respect that, for now.

"Well, I came by to say hello to my new neighbor and apologize ahead of time for the noise you'll be living with for the next month or so. I was also hoping to place a standing order for fresh flowers every week for my café."

She set the cup down on the desk and stared at me. "What are you talking about? Who is your neighbor? And I'd be happy to make you a standing order of flowers, but I'm not sure how I would get them to Rochester."

I picked up her hands and gave them a squeeze. "You're my new neighbor, and I think you can manage to get me flowers since I'll be next door."

If I had a camera, I would have taken a picture at the very instant it hit her. Instead, I was grabbing a chair for her to sit in when she started trembling under my hands.

"You bought Buck's?" she questioned, her voice high pitched and squeaky.

I knelt next to her, concern for her wellbeing outweighing anything else in my mind. "Savannah, you're scaring me."

"I'm okay, really, I am. I'm just shocked. Buck's. Wow."

I rested my elbow on my knee and grinned at

her. "I wasn't expecting shock and awe," I teased. "I was hoping you would be excited that we're going to be neighbors."

"I am excited. Snowberry needs a café, and you're the perfect person to get one up and running successfully here. I just feel terrible for Buck and Nana."

She cried out, and her face contorted. She bent forward and grabbed her cheek as she rocked in the chair.

"Savannah, you have to breathe. Breathe through it like Snow taught you," I encouraged her.

She gasped and kept rocking, the rise and fall of her chest quick and uneven, but at least she was breathing. I rubbed her back and tried to keep her calm until the spasm passed. When it did, she was exhausted and barely had the strength to sit upright in the chair. I glanced at my watch. It was nearly three, and she usually didn't close until seven. I peeked at her again and made an executive decision. She was going home.

"Will you be okay if I leave for a minute? I'll be right back." I promised, and she nodded weakly.

I jogged out of the room and grabbed a piece of paper from under the counter in the front, scribbling a note on it. I stuck it to the front door with a bit of floral tape on the way to my truck, ignoring the ice patches as I slipped across the street to fire it up. Once it was in front of her door, I put the heat on full blast. The street was deserted, and I was thankful I didn't have to worry about anyone messing with a running vehicle in this town.

By the time I got back inside the emporium, Savannah was coming out from the back room. She was using whatever she could find to hold herself up as she walked across the room. In four strides, I had her in my arms, and in four more had her inside my truck, seatbelt buckled. I went back inside and got her purse, coat, and keys, shut off the lights, and flipped the closed sign over. One last pull on the door assured me it was locked. I climbed back in the truck and buckled up.

“I can’t do this anymore, Noel. I’ve got nothing left,” she murmured then fell into an exhausted sleep.

I put the truck in gear and pulled away from the curb, hoping I could remember the way to her house.

"I understand, Snow. I'll do my best to keep her quiet for the rest of the night," I promised the woman on the other end of the line. After I got Savannah home, and in bed, her best friend had called. She also happens to be a doctor, so I asked her advice on the matter. "If she has another attack, I'll call you immediately and then take her to the ER."

"Savan was lucky you were there today," Snow said.

I blew out a breath. "I think I probably caused it. I told her I was buying Buck's. She got upset that Buck had to sell, and that's when the spasm hit."

"Don't blame yourself, Noel. Her face has gone downhill a lot over the last few months. She's being stubborn and refusing to see the specialist, so there isn't much any of us can do. You're not to blame for the situation. That said, I can't believe you bought Buck's! I'm so excited!" she squealed.

I laughed then, and the simple action relaxed my chest again. "Thank you, that's the first time I've told someone and gotten excitement as their first reaction."

"Are you going to make it a café?"

"You betcha. As soon as I sign the papers, I'll bring in a team to remodel the dining room. I hope to have it open in a month or so."

"That's so awesome, Noel. Snowberry really needs a place where families can eat out and where kids can gather. You're going to be welcomed here with open arms."

I smiled a little, feeling for the first time like someone else saw the potential in my café. "I already do feel welcome here, that's why I chose Snowberry for the next café. It was time to do something new while reconnecting with December. I want to be here the day she and Jay have their first baby, and I want to be here to give that baby his or her first job. It's important to me that I'm here for her after deserting her for so many years."

Snow sighed a little. "I can't wait for the day

they have their first little one either, but meanwhile, I can borrow you a little one to be an uncle to if you so desire."

I chuckled and nodded my head. "Sunny is pretty hard to say no to already. I can't imagine another, but I'm always here if you need anything, and I mean that."

"I know you do, Noel. You and December are the right stuff, and right now, I need you to watch over my bestie."

"You got it. I'll send you a text later when she's up. Thanks for the advice." I told her goodbye and hit the off button, laying it on the counter.

I glanced around the quaint home and thought about the last time I was here. It was Christmas Eve, and I was in Snowberry for December's wedding. I stayed later than I originally planned and was invited back for Christmas Day, which was grand, but I had no place to stay. There was literally no room in the inn.

Savannah offered me her guest room, and I gladly accepted. The house was a 1950's bungalow style with an open floor plan kitchen and dining area. The front sitting room looked out over the yard and sported an impressive stone fireplace with wood mantle. The bedrooms were situated at each end of a long hallway with the bathroom in the middle. The basement was full, completely renovated, and made a great rec room.

I stood in the kitchen, which had recently been redone, and had every amenity at your fingertips.

Savannah had been sleeping for a few hours, and I was manning her phone, even if she didn't know it. I scribbled her cell phone number on the sheet of paper as an emergency number and stuck it to the door of the shop. Thankfully, no one had called with a flower emergency.

She would need dinner when she got up, so I opened the fridge and dug around. In fifteen seconds, I was frowning. Does the woman ever eat? I opened the freezer and my frown deepened. It was full to the brim with frozen dinners. I guess she ate, but she sure didn't eat anything good.

I rummaged around the boxes in the freezer, moving stuff aside, but all I came up with were two frozen pork chops. It was a start. I set them on the counter and opened the fridge again. The meat drawer held some cheese that still smelled okay, and the vegetable drawer had four carrots and three potatoes. I grabbed them all out and set the pathetic lot on the stove.

I started opening cupboards next and came up with a packet of dried onion soup mix and some cornstarch. Things are looking up. It wouldn't be gourmet, but it would be comfort food.

It wasn't my usual recipe for pork stew, but I guess a guy had to work with what he had. I rinsed the vegetables and set them on the cutting board, digging around for a knife. Once they were ready, I dumped the cut vegetables into the cooking pot and put the lid on, turning the burner to low so it could simmer.

There was movement in the hallway, and I put the cutting board in the sink just as Savannah stepped into the room. Except for her apron, she was still dressed in her work clothes. Her hair stuck up on one side, and her eyes were red.

"Noel, you're still here," she said, surprised.

"I am." I smiled and leaned on the counter. "I would never leave a friend in need."

She gave me half a smile and sat on the edge of a bar stool. "I'm sorry to take up so much of your day. I'm all right, really. You can go."

I scooted around the island and stood in front of her. "You haven't taken up my day, but you are a liar, and I'm not going anywhere."

She looked at me with fire in her eyes, but she didn't refute my words. I took her shoulders and guided her to the hallway, stopping in front of the bathroom.

"Why don't you take a shower while dinner is on the stove? Climb into some comfy, warm clothes, and then come eat with me. I'll make you some coffee," I encouraged.

She glanced up at me and nodded, biting her lip. "I don't have much food here. I don't really cook."

"I noticed," I teased, her face turning red. "I found enough to make a pot of Noel Kiss stew, so don't fret."

She put her hand on the door to the bathroom. "I'll be out in twenty minutes, but don't make me any coffee, it makes my face worse."

"Okay, no coffee."

I smiled and she returned it before she disappeared behind the door.

Chapter Three

I sat in the chair opposite her and watched her pick at the few pieces of potato and carrot left in her bowl. When she finished her shower, she was happy and smiling, but she was also acting like the last five hours hadn't happened. I let it go through dinner, and we talked about my plans for the café, the Minnesota Vikings terrible season, and her business preparations for the upcoming Valentine's Day holiday. As the meal came to an end, her mood turned somber again.

"If you're full, you don't have to eat more on my account."

She gazed up at me and nodded. "It was delicious, but I'm full. I still can't believe you made this from the little bit you could find around here," she marveled.

"I grew up in a restaurant, making something from nothing is called the blue plate special."

She laughed a little and tipped her head to the side. "Well, this blue-plate special was outstanding. Thank you, but I can't eat another bite."

I picked up the dishes and carried everything to the sink. From the corner of my eye, I noticed she had wandered into the living room to gaze out the window. Something was definitely on her mind, and if I couldn't get it out of her, then I was going to have to call Snow to come over and talk to her. I ran some water in the dishes and left them in the sink, walking into the living room where she was still standing.

"If you want to talk about it, I'm more than happy to listen," I said, laying my hand on her arm.

She jumped a little but kept her eyes locked on the shadows in the yard. "In a nutshell, I'm going to lose my house because I can't afford to live here anymore."

Her shoulders sagged, and she crossed her arms over her chest. I could tell it was the first time she'd said it out loud, and suddenly, that made it real.

I wrapped my arm around her shoulder and walked her to the couch, helping her to sit. I sat next to her and took her hand. "I'm sorry, Savannah. Would you like me to call Snow?"

She shook her head and stared down at her hands. "No, I don't want to bother or worry her. She's pregnant and doesn't need to concern herself with my problems."

I turned her chin until she faced me. "That's what friends are for. She's already worried sick about you. I talked to her earlier."

She jumped up and threw her arms up in the air in anger. "Oh, great, so now you're reporting to my mommy? That's fantastic. Thanks for sticking your nose in where it doesn't belong, Noel."

She dropped her hands and stomped to the hallway, where she promptly sank to her knees. Her tantrum was forgotten immediately, and by the time I got to her, she was retching, her face contorted. I grabbed the wastebasket and held it while she vomited, the agony of it causing tears to leak from her eyes. When it passed, she was ashen and shaking. I picked her up, carried her to the couch, and found a washcloth in the bathroom for her head.

"I'm going to take you to the hospital. Snow said if you had any more attacks tonight, I should bring you in."

I didn't even care that she was already mad about me talking to Snow, I was too scared. I couldn't imagine how she must be feeling.

She held onto my shirt tightly. "No, please, I'm okay. I've been too worked up today. If I don't get worked up, the spasms don't happen. I promise."

I stuck my leg out in front of me and sat down on the floor. "I won't apologize for talking to Snow. She called, and I answered your phone. I left your number on the sign at the shop, so I thought it might be a client. Snow was worried the second I answered the phone. You can't pull anything over on that woman. I told her what happened, but nothing more."

She closed her eyes and swallowed then, nodding at my words. "Would you make me some tea? There's a box of it by the Keurig machine."

"Of course." I stood up and went to the kitchen. I located the box of chamomile tea and stuck a pod in the machine. While it brewed, I took an ice pack from the freezer and wrapped it in a towel for her face.

The machine finished brewing and said, *Enjoy,* but something told me she wouldn't be enjoying anything for a while. By the time I got back to the living room, she was upright on the couch, and I handed her the tea and then the ice pack.

"I thought maybe it would help by numbing your face a little? Or does that just make it worse?" I didn't know what I was doing, but I wanted to help her any way I could.

She took a sip of the tea and held the ice pack to her face. "Sometimes it helps by numbing it. Thank you. I'm sorry for being a jerk a few minutes ago. I'm having a hard time right now."

I sat next to her on the couch and rubbed her arm. "No apology needed. You're obviously stressed out, which is understandable. Is the house issue what I walked in on this afternoon?"

She sighed. "I was just looking at the books and trying to figure out a way to make the mortgage payment on the shop and the house tomorrow. The math just doesn't add up. I knew my savings wasn't going to last long, but I didn't want to admit it. I let my last employee go a few months back, but even that hasn't helped. I love this little house, and I don't want to give it up."

"Is business that bad?" I asked, trying to figure

out why suddenly she was having problems making both payments.

"No, the business can more than support me and the building, but when we bought this house, Günther was helping make the house payment."

"Günther? Is that your ex?"

She laughed without mirth. "That would be him."

"How long ago did he leave?"

"He left the first time over two years ago."

"The first time?"

"We separated because he had anger issues, and I was afraid of him. We were apart for almost six months, and he was going to counseling. He swore he was a changed man. He wanted another chance and I agreed, don't ask me why. I knew I didn't love him anymore, I was just, I don't know, I felt like I should give it one more shot. Anyway, he was here for about three months, and, well, it didn't work out."

"Savannah, did he do this to your face?" I asked, pulling the ice pack down.

"I suppose his actions were the inciting factor."

"He hit you." What I tried to make a question came out a statement. I read the truth in her eyes and it made my stomach revolt.

"Hit, punched, kicked, you name it. I should never have let him back in the house, but to be honest, I wanted to believe he had changed. I wanted to believe he loved me and couldn't live without me. It didn't take two days to see he hadn't changed, two more to see he didn't love me, and two more before the first punch was thrown. I lasted two more months and filed for divorce. This was his parting gift." She motioned at her face.

"Why didn't you press charges, Savannah?"

"I was afraid he would kill me if I did. He made it very clear in his fits of rage what he would do to me if I went to the police. When he got the divorce papers, he signed them, and I never heard from him again."

"When was that?" I asked softly.

"A year ago on Thanksgiving."

"You've suffered from this for over a year?" I asked, shocked.

"No, it didn't start until about Halloween this year. I thought the injury had healed, and everything was fine."

"How did it happen?"

There was no question by my tone that I was demanding an answer.

"When I asked him to leave, he punched me in the eye." She closed her right one and put the icepack over it. "I'm pretty sure he cracked the socket when he struck me, but I refused to seek treatment."

I swallowed and held tight to her other hand. "After it healed, it didn't bother you like this?"

"If I'm honest with myself, then I would have to say it did bother me. It hurt all the time. I had a constant ache that left me exhausted by the end of the day. I took bottles of Tylenol and Advil, but nothing helped. The doctor Snow made me see in the ER said that's because it's a nerve. She made me go to the ER right before December's wedding. He said it was the result of facial trauma, even though it didn't start until months later."

"Now, the pain is getting worse," I surmised.

"Only if I'm stressed, otherwise I can control it," she jumped in, but I could tell even she didn't believe that lie.

I changed the subject, so she didn't get worked up again. "When you got divorced, didn't you have to sell the house?"

"We did, or else I had to buy out his half. I knew I was stretching it, but I had already lost so much. I didn't want to give up my home. He hated this house, but it was the first place I'd ever felt at home," she lamented. "I just don't know what I'm going to do or where I'm going to go."

I rubbed her arm, and she laid her head on my shoulder. "How much do you need to make the house payment tomorrow?"

"The whole payment, about six hundred."

I stood up and went to my suit jacket, pulling out my checkbook. I wrote a check to her and brought it over. "I'll take you to the bank in the morning so you can make sure the payment gets there on time."

She glanced down at the check and then back up at me. "Noel, no. I can't take your money. Thank you, but no, I can't."

I sat back down next to her and took her hand.

"Consider it payment for letting me use your guest room the last few times. I haven't exactly made a reservation either time."

She was still shaking her head when she spoke. "You don't need a reservation, but no, it's too much. I'm a thirty-two-year-old woman who ought to be able to pay her own bills. I just need to realize that I have to let the house go. If I let it go into default now, then I can live here until spring when I can find an apartment. There's nothing available right now, I've already looked."

"Honey, you're a thirty-two-year-old woman who started a successful business and helps her friends out whenever they need it, even when their twenty-six-year-old brother deposits himself on your doorstep." I winked, and she laughed a little. "You've also been dealt a hard hand to play, and you're still dealing pretty darn well."

"That's for sure," she whispered, dropping the ice pack to her lap.

"You've brought up an excellent point, which I hadn't thought about, but one that is now going to leave me in a lurch," I admitted, tapping my finger on my jaw.

I stood and walked to the window, looking out at the beautiful snow glistening under the streetlight. "I'm moving here to start a business, but there are no apartments for rent?"

"None. There aren't a lot of rentals to start with in Snowberry and ..." She just tossed up her hand to end the sentence.

"Maybe we can help each other out then," I suggested. She sat up as I joined her back on the couch. "I need a place to stay, and you need someone to help you pay the mortgage, right?" She nodded but I could see in her eyes she was scared of what I was about to say. "What if I rent your spare room? I promise to put the seat down, make sure my laundry is never on the floor, and I'll do the grocery shopping and cooking."

"Are you sure?"

The way she looked at me said she wondered if I was her savior.

"I'm only sure of one thing, Savannah. Moving to Snowberry was never in my plans until I met you. Since Christmas Eve, I haven't been able to think about anything else. When I found Buck's today, it felt like divine intervention. Let me help you over this bump in the road. I promise not to encroach on your space or ask anything from you. It's the perfect answer to both of our problems."

She glanced down at the check and back at me. "I guess it's true what they say. Sometimes fate intervenes in a way you'd never expect."

Chapter Four

I glanced in my side mirror to check the small trailer behind the truck for the tenth time since leaving Rochester. After I signed the paperwork Wednesday and took ownership of the building, I drove back to Rochester to talk with Nick. He was more than ready to take control of the café and run with it. In fact, all he did was smile slyly, shake my hand, and salute me. Surprisingly, when I walked out the door of the café, I didn't feel like I was leaving anything behind. I was confident I was discovering the rest of my life. It was a compelling and overwhelming feeling.

All I had to do was think about the look in Savannah's eyes when she realized she could stay in her home, and I wanted to race right back to her. Before I could do that, I had to figure out what to do with my childhood home.

I stood in the middle of it yesterday, wondering how far to take this new adventure. The house had been in our family for generations, and it didn't feel right to put it on the market. I was starting a new life, but I couldn't stand to part with the last piece of Mom and Dad that I had left. Deccy was staying in Snowberry and I truly believed I would be too, but I hesitated to sell it. It was paid for, so keeping it over the winter wasn't a big deal. Something was telling me not to worry about it until spring.

The problem was getting it winterized for the harsh Minnesota winter. When Nick showed up at my doorstep to help me load the trailer, he could tell I was distracted.

He got us a beer, and I shared my dilemma. It was like the answer was sitting right in front of me and I asked him to take care of the house. All he had to do was make sure the pipes didn't freeze, and the sidewalks were shoveled. I offered to pay him, but he said he could do one better if I was willing.

Nick's apartment complex was about to be torn down to make room for another parking garage. He had to move out by the end of the month and hadn't found a place. I didn't even hesitate. I stood up, handed him the key, and thanked him for solving my problem. He laughed and said I was the lifesaver, but he really had no idea how much weight was off my shoulders to know my family home was in good hands. He insisted on paying rent, but I finally convinced him if he paid the utilities and taxes on the place, he could live there rent-free for the cost of the upkeep. I'm not sure who was happier about the agreement, him or me, but either way, when I drove away today, I had no worries about my café or my house.

I didn't take much with me other than my personal belongings. Savannah's house was already cozy, and I didn't see much need to drag along a lot of things I wouldn't use. I packed the trailer with equipment and furnishings for the new café, along with a few items of our mother's, to give December.

After my parents died, and I shut December out of my life, I packed up all of their belongings and moved them to the basement. There were photo albums, my mother's china, and other family heirlooms I knew she would love to have. If offering her a few things from our past helped build our future, I was more than willing to move it the hour north with me.

My phone buzzed in my ear, and I snapped out of my daydreams to answer. "This is Noel."

"Hey, Noel, this is Big Eddie. We ran into a snag here," his voice boomed, and I cringed when the Bluetooth nearly blew my eardrum out.

"What's the problem, Eddie?" I asked the foreman of the construction team.

"I can't make that door work the way you wanted. We ran into a stud wall. To put the door there, I would have to rebuild the wall, but it's a load-bearing one," he explained. I tapped my fingers on the steering wheel. "We can put it around back with a ramp if that works."

I shook my head, "No, that doesn't work. I'm not putting a handicapped door in the back of the building. That insinuates that disabled people don't deserve to use the front door," I ground out, my head starting to hurt.

"You're the boss, man. Have any other ideas?" he asked, his gum snapping as the air blew threw his phone, whistling in my ear.

I thought about it for a few moments. "Where the door is now, can we utilize that space at all?"

"Hang tight, I'll call you back," he said, and the line went dead. I rolled my eyes a little and pulled into town. I had planned to go right to Savannah's but turned toward the town square instead.

I would rather talk to Big Eddie myself than have him howling in my ear again for ten minutes. When I pulled up across the street from the café, it looked like a construction trailer had exploded. I had never seen so much equipment strewn across the entire sidewalk before. I was going to be the number one hated neighbor if I didn't do something fast.

I jumped from the truck and grabbed my jacket, jogging across the street and up onto the curb. Big Eddie was standing with his hands on his hips, his tool-belt pulling his pants dangerously low, and a scowl on his face.

"Hey, Big Eddie, I was just pulling into town and thought I'd swing by," I explained, jogging up to him.

He stuck his hand out, and I shook it, his big beefy hand nearly crushing mine. "Good to see ya, boss. Just trying to work out some plans for this here door."

I motioned around the sidewalk. "Uh, listen, Eddie, is there any way we can move this to the back of the café?"

He turned and looked at the saws and tools littering the sidewalk. "Move what?"

I tried not to growl my answer. "All the tools and the trailers. I have to think about being a good neighbor to the other businesses here, even while the place is under construction. There is plenty of space in the back for this stuff."

He stared at me like I had horns on my head. "It's true, boss, but there's no door back there. I can't ask my guys to be lugging heavy stuff all the way around the front."

Great, this is the time he chooses to use logic.

"Let's take a walk." I motioned, heading around the side of the building.

The café sat on the corner lot, and the sidewalk went around the side and ended in a small empty lot in the back of the building. The lot had recently been blacktopped but had nothing else going for it. The back of the building was an open canvas and I stood there, my hand on my hip. I put my back to the building and gazed out over nothing but pastureland for as far as the eye could see. I turned around again and rubbed my hands together to fight off the cold.

"You know, what if we made this the main entrance to the building?" I asked, and he glanced at me then back to the building.

"Boss, you just said you didn't want to do that."

"No, I said I don't want the handicapped ramp in the back while everyone else used the front door. I have absolutely no problem with making this the main entrance. It would open up the front of the building, and we could leave that door as an emergency exit. If we don't need a bigger door there, we have room for a large window instead. There's plenty of parking back here, and we have room for a door and ramp that are up to code for the ADA."

I stepped back a couple of feet and stuck my hands in my pockets. "This whole side of the building," I said, indicating the left side, "could be the door. We put a double-sided sign with the café name, and we put up a *parking in back* sign. Then we're set. Does that solve the door problem?"

"Yessiree, it sure does," he admitted, rubbing his jaw. "Let me go fill the guys in. They're just demoing stuff right now, so we haven't done any work that will be wasted. I'll be sure to get all the stuff moved back here, too," he assured me as we walked around the front of the building.

"Great, thanks, Eddie. I'm going to go drop this trailer off, but if you need anything, just call," I encouraged him.

He shook my hand and disappeared inside the café. I hesitated on the sidewalk, trying to decide if I should stop in at the emporium or go to her house. Before I made the conscious decision, my feet were already moving to the door, and my hand was pulling it open. The smell of fresh gardenias hit me when I walked in and I smiled. That was the scent that Savannah always wore when she walked by me. Today, it wasn't Savannah behind the counter.

"Hello, you're not Savannah," I said to the girl by the cash register.

She smiled brightly and shook her head. "No, I'm April."

I stuck my hand out across the counter, "Nice to meet you, April. I'm Noel Kiss. Where is Savannah?"

"At home, I believe. She said she would be back in a few hours." Her voice was guttural, and I had to concentrate on what she said.

I checked my watch, and it was a little past noon. I grabbed a bouquet of the gardenias and handed them to her. "I'll take these then." I smiled and hoped I looked friendly and not crazy.

"These are beautiful. They're so fragrant I almost feel like it's spring. A lucky lady is about to be had." She grinned, putting them in a protective bag and taking the cash I held out.

"It was nice to meet you, April, I'm sure I'll see you around. I just bought Buck's next door, and will be opening a café next month," I explained.

Her face lit up with recognition. "So, you're the guy who's bringing home-cooking back to Snowberry. I hope you're ready for an onslaught when you open. People can barely contain their excitement and wonderment about the place."

I rocked back on my heels and grinned. "Well,

that's good to hear. Nothing like knowing you have a ready and willing customer base before you even open the doors. If you're looking for any extra work, stop on over. Let others know, too. I need a workforce."

"Oh, I will, Mr. Kiss. Thank you," she gushed.

I chuckled a little. "Just call me Noel. Hey, maybe you can help me out, actually. The building isn't going to be ready for at least a month, but I will need to do a hiring day. Do you have any idea where I might be able to have one of those, and how to get the word out?"

"I sure do. If you want to stop back in a few hours, I will have all of that information for you."

"I can do that. Let me go drop off my trailer at my new place. I'm glad I stopped in today, April. I think you and I will be good friends."

She waved shyly. "Snowberry is a friendly place, Noel. We welcome newcomers and want you to succeed. Let me put some feelers out. I'm sure Savannah won't mind."

"I know she won't mind. I'm sure she appreciates that you could come in to help. I'll be back in a bit."

I waved and pulled the door open. A shiver ran through me, and I tried to tell myself it was from the cold, but my heart knew otherwise. If Savannah wasn't here, that meant she was in trouble.

When I pulled up to Savannah's house, her car was in the driveway. I pulled the truck forward and blocked her in with the trailer. This assured me she wouldn't be able to leave until we talked. My heart was pounding in my chest the whole way here because something was off, way off. Savannah didn't leave the emporium in just anyone's hands, and she didn't have enough revenue to pay an employee.

I grabbed the railing on the stairs and jogged up the few steps to the door. I was getting ready to knock when she opened the door.

"You have a key." She pointed at my raised hand.

I dropped it to my side. "I know, but I wasn't expecting you to be home, so I didn't want to interrupt something."

She motioned me in, and I stepped through the door, trying to get a good look at her, but she moved away quickly.

"I had to stop at the café and answer a question for Big Eddie. While I was there, I stopped in at the shop and met April," I told her, slipping my jacket off and laying it on the couch. "She seems nice."

She paused on her way into the kitchen and nodded. "She's a sweet girl. I know her mom, and she said April was looking for work. I offered to have her work a few hours here and there for me until she can find something else."

I stood behind her and put my hand on her

shoulder. "Can you afford to pay someone else to work, Savannah?"

"Don't worry about my business, Noel. I have things under control," she snapped.

I turned her to me, but she refused to meet my eyes. "I'm not worried about your business. I'm worried about you. I know you don't like leaving the emporium."

"I just needed a break, Noel. I'm about to head over there now. If you move the trailer, I'll get out of the way so you can move your stuff in," she mumbled, trying to push past me.

I tilted her chin up toward me, but she resisted the motion and stepped around me. I grabbed her arm and held her there.

"Please, let go of me," she cried. She wrenched her arm from my hand, ran to the living room, and threw on her coat.

"Savannah, wait," I ordered, taking her arm again, but she fought against me and pushed me back against the couch.

"I said, don't touch me," she screamed, then ran out the front door.

My mind was trying to catch up with her reaction, but my body was already moving out the door. She was in her car, and I jumped behind it, bracing my hands on the trunk.

"Savannah, I'm sorry. I just wanted to talk to you. I didn't mean to scare you," I yelled, hoping she could hear me inside the car. I knew she could see me because the car hadn't moved into reverse.

"You have to at least let me move my truck."

The window slid down, and I went to the driver's side door. "Please, come in and talk to me for a few minutes. April didn't seem to be in a hurry to go anywhere."

She nodded and sighed before she put the window up. The engine cut off, and I pulled the door handle to open the door. She climbed out and walked past me without a glance. When we finally got into the house, I took her coat from her shoulders and hung it on the coat rack. When I turned back around, she was dabbing at her eye with a tissue.

My heart sank, knowing I was the one to make her cry. "I didn't mean to make you cry, forgive me," I said softly and sincerely. "It was insensitive of me to grab you. I promise it won't happen again."

"You didn't make me cry," she corrected, finally looking up. Her right eye was pointing at the floor, and the lid had fallen over it, leaving just a slit for her to see out of. It was watering at a steady rate, making it appear as though she was crying. What disturbed me the most was the fact that the whole right side of her face was completely paralyzed.

I led her to the couch and pulled her down next to me, tugging off her stocking cap. "When did this start? It wasn't like this Wednesday."

"When I woke up this morning, this is what I looked like. I thought it might have been because it was swollen. I've used ice, taken Advil, and given it time, but there's been no improvement. I guess this is just what it's going to be like from now on."

"Does it hurt?" I asked, trying to get a little better look at it.

"Exquisitely tender. The ice and ibuprofen helped that, but it didn't help the muscle movement."

I could tell because some of her words slurred when she spoke. "Have you called Snow?"

She shook her head no, which wasn't a surprise.

"I want to call her. Will you let me?" I asked, not wanting to upset her like I did the last time.

She shrugged, and half-nodded, so I took that as a yes and quickly dialed Snow's number. She picked up on the second ring and was on guard immediately.

"Is there a problem, Noel?"

"I think so, that's why I'm calling you," I answered, smiling at Savannah.

I filled Snow in on the latest developments while I held Savannah's hand. Once I agreed to her terms, I clicked the phone off and stuck it in my pocket.

"Let's go for a little ride. Snow wants to see you." I smiled, but she didn't even attempt to smile back.

"No, I can't afford to go to the ER. I don't have insurance."

I stood up and took her coat back down off the rack, then helped her up. "She said you'd say that.

Her answer was to go straight to her office. Dr. Snow has no charge appointments today."

She rolled her one eye, but the other stayed pointed down. As disturbing as it was to see, it was more disturbing to know someone who was supposed to love her did this to her.

I helped her back into her coat and locked the door behind me as we walked to the truck. I gave her a hand into the truck and then quickly unhooked the trailer, rolling it into the driveway. When I climbed in, the truck was still warm, but she had her stocking cap pulled down over half her face and was staring at her shoes. I put it into gear and pulled out onto the street, then slipped my hand across the seat and took hers.

"I can't promise you everything's going to be okay, but I can promise you that I won't leave your side," I whispered.

I was rewarded with a soft squeeze to my hand, and that was all I needed.

Chapter Five

I parked the truck in the hospital parking lot, and she unbuckled her seatbelt. "Thanks for the ride, Noel. You don't have to stay. I'll walk to the shop when I'm done."

I lightly grasped the arm of her coat and stopped her as she reached for the door handle. "The hospital is over a mile away from the emporium. If you want to go to the shop after you see Snow, I'll drive you, but I'm staying."

"I don't want to take up all of your time. You have things to do, and tomorrow is Jay and December's reception."

"I already stopped in and talked to Big Eddie. He's got things under control. The only other thing I have to do right now is to take you up to see Dr. Snow, who, by the way, scares me a little bit. I really don't want her mad at me."

She started to giggle. "That little thing scares you? You're twice her size."

"That may well be true, but have you met her? She's scary smart, not to mention commanding. Her size doesn't cross my mind when she's giving orders. So, let's not anger the little thing, and just do as she says." I winked, and she smiled, but only one side of her face went up. I ran my hand down the left side of her face until she nodded under my hand.

I hopped out of the truck and helped her down out of the big F150 that made her look even smaller than she was. She leaned the right side of her face on my shoulder as we walked in the front doors, and I knew it was so no one would see her face. The hospital was bustling, and I walked her to the elevator quickly, before anyone could stop us.

I didn't mind having her arm around my waist and her stocking cap clad head tucked under my chin. It was nice to be needed, and not just to solve a problem at the café. To really be needed on an emotional level was something I hadn't experienced often in my life. It was mostly my own doing, considering I distanced myself from everyone after my mom died. I was so busy running the cafes, I didn't realize how much I needed to feel love until December wrapped her arms around me after our long absence ended. Now, I was making up for lost time.

"What floor is she on?" I asked, and she punched the button for the third floor without speaking. We rode up in silence. I would like to say she was relaxed in my arms, but she was stiff as a board. When the doors slid open, I practically had to drag her down the hallway to Snow's office.

I raised my arm to knock and heard, *come in*, instead. "She's a Jedi," I whispered into Savannah's ear, and I was rewarded with a snicker.

When I pushed the door open, Snow was behind her desk, its imposing cherry wood making her look even smaller than her usual pixie size. I was glad when she wheeled her wheelchair toward us. She took Savannah's hand, immediately directing her to a chair without saying a word. Savannah sat, and Snow pulled her hat off, letting it fall to her lap.

"Oh, Savan." She sighed, and Savannah threw her arms around Snow and cried.

"I'll be outside."

I motioned to the hallway, and Snow, who was patting Savannah's back, glanced up at me.

"There's a room four doors down with a fridge. Would you grab a bottle of water for her?" she asked.

I nodded and slipped from the room to give them some privacy. I found the small breakroom and grabbed a bottle of water from the fridge. I took a moment and a deep breath before I went back to her office.

What am I doing here? A few weeks ago, I didn't know any of these people even existed. Now, I've bought a restaurant and moved in with a woman I've only met twice. A beautiful woman who was in a lot of pain. That's what I was doing here.

I closed my eyes and breathed in. I was here to help Savannah in any way that I could. After a deep breath, there was a decrease in my anxiety and I opened my eyes. I was born to be hers, of that, I had no doubt.

I grabbed the bottle of water off the table and jogged back down the hallway, pushing the door open far enough to sneak a look inside. Snow was testing Savannah's vision, and I brought the water bottle in and set it on the desk. Savannah had pulled herself together and was doing what Snow asked without argument. I sat in a chair off to the side and waited through the rest of Snow's exam.

"I'm concerned," Snow finally said, handing Savannah the water. "Dr. Thompson warned you that this might happen. He said if it did, you were going to need decompression surgery on that nerve."

Savannah lowered the water bottle slowly and nodded. "I know what he said."

"Who is Dr. Thompson? Can he help her?" I asked, and Snow shook her head negatively.

"Dr. Thompson is the ER doc she saw before December's wedding. The only doctor who can help her now is in Rochester at Mayo."

"Can you get her an appointment?" I asked. Snow nodded, her eyes darting to Savannah, who was shaking her head.

"No, no appointment. You know I don't have insurance. I can't afford Mayo or any other hospital. I'll figure something out, but I can't afford surgery right now."

Snow sighed and rolled behind her desk. "Be that as it may, I'm still concerned, and you still have a problem. I'm going to write you a prescription for prednisone to help relieve the swelling around the nerve. I'm afraid to do a cortisone injection and cause more damage, so it's our only option right now."

Savannah was shaking her head. "I can't take that. Remember what happened the last time? My heart got full of water."

I whipped my head around and stared at Snow. "Heart full of water?" That didn't sound good at all.

Snow laid her pen down. "The prednisone made her retain water, and the fluid built up around her heart, but she was on a massive dose of it. This time, I'm giving her a tiny dose every day and a water pill to take with it, so she doesn't retain any water. It's a temporary measure until we can figure out what to do. It will get her through the weekend and the reception since I know she has to do all the flowers for the hall."

Snow picked her pen back up to finish the prescriptions, and I sat down next to Savannah. "Do you have to do all the flowers for tomorrow yet?"

She nodded and grimaced a little, at least as much as her paralyzed face let her. "Yeah, that's why I have to get to the shop. I always do big events like weddings and such after hours, so I'm not interrupted. It will be a late-night but I'll get them done."

"I'll help. I may not know a lot about flowers, but I can move and carry things as you finish them. I can also help you get them to the hall in the morning for set up. Does April know how to do the arranging?"

She gave me the so-so hand. "Not really, besides, I can't afford to pay her now that she's been there all day today."

"Then it's you and me, kid." I winked, and she opened her mouth to object, but I laid my finger on her lips. "No arguments."

Snow snorted, and I fought at the smile on my lips. Savannah not arguing about accepting help, was like a bear not stealing a pot of honey, but she quieted and sat next to me resigned.

"Here are the prescriptions." Snow handed them across the desk, and I took them from her. "Any pharmacy can fill them."

"How much will they cost?" Savannah asked immediately.

Snow sighed heavily. "Less than ten bucks for both of them. Please, get them filled, Savannah, it's all I can do for you right now."

I tucked them in the inside of my coat pocket and stood. "I'll drop her off at the emporium and get them filled right away, not to worry, Snow."

Snow smiled at me gratefully. "Thanks, Noel."

She rolled around her desk and took her friend's hand. "If your pain gets worse, you start seeing double, or you get a migraine, you have to call me. Got it?"

Savannah nodded, giving her half a salute, and Snow pulled her into a hug that had nothing to do with being a doctor and everything to do with being a best friend who was scared to death.

I leaned against the bar with a beer in one hand and my eyes on the dance floor. If nothing else, my sister knows how to throw a party. The dance was in full swing, and people were doing a line dance to an old country song.

After we left Snow's office yesterday, I took Savannah to the shop and then went to the pharmacy to get her prescriptions filled. While I was there, I searched the aisles until I came up with a solution for what she felt was the reason she couldn't come to the party tonight. She begrudgingly took the pills when I brought them back to the shop, and cried when I gave her the floral print eye coverings, and a gift certificate to get her hair done today at Crow's Hair and Nails.

My eyes drifted to where she sat at the table. She was playing some kind of hand rhythm game with Sunny. Her eye was covered with the patch, and her hair fell down across it in such a way you didn't even notice something was amiss.

All I saw was how beautiful she looked in a sky blue dress that hugged her every curve, and brushed the floor when she walked. It had taken me longer than I cared to admit to control my longings when she came out of the bedroom tonight. She was drop-dead gorgeous and I had to remind myself that I had to control my anger toward the man who put her in so much pain.

The pain was relentless, often leaving her breathless and curled up in a ball. The intensity of the attacks left no doubt that she wouldn't be able to live with them indefinitely. I was going to have to figure out a way to help her before it was too late.

Last night, we worked late, and by the time we finished, I could tell she was in pain. She could barely lift her chin off her chest by the time I got her in the truck and back to the house. She went to bed with an icepack and a promise that she would come get me if she needed anything. I spent the rest of the night unpacking the trailer of my personal effects and thinking about the things she had told me while we were working at the emporium.

She was resilient, but she was still afraid Günther would turn up and destroy what was left of her life. I guess that was a natural fear if you'd been controlled by someone like him for years. She was furious with him and her own choices, not that his inability to control his anger was her fault. With one well-placed punch, he left his mark on her, maybe for the rest of her life. There was nothing fair about that kind of reality. When I asked her if she ever saw a counselor, she just shrugged her shoulder, which was enough of an answer. She hadn't, and she didn't intend to.

The lights went down, and the music changed

to a slow song. I set my beer on the bar and pushed off it, running my hands over my pants. Sunny had run off to dance with her daddy, and Savannah sat alone in the shadows at the table. I held my hand out to her. “May I have this dance?”

She glanced up and smiled but shook her head. “You don’t have to dance with me, Noel. I’m okay here.”

I didn’t drop my hand. “I know I don’t have to dance with you, but I want to. Honestly, I’m feeling a little self-conscious standing here with my hand out.”

She closed her eye but reached out and put her hand in mine. “I wouldn’t want you to feel self-conscious. Promise me no complicated moves. It’s hard to stay coordinated when I can only see out of one eye,” she whispered as I drew her into me.

We were close, my arm around her waist and my lips near her ear. “I don’t plan on making any moves you aren’t ready for me to make. Dancing slow is okay, it keeps you close to me.”

She laid her head against my shoulder, and if she caught my innuendo, she didn’t let on. “You’re beautiful, have I told you that tonight? I love what Crow did with your hair.”

She nodded against my lapel. “You’ve mentioned it a couple of times, thank you. Crow is a bit of a miracle worker.”

“You think Crow’s handiwork is why you’re beautiful tonight? You’re wrong. I think you’re beautiful every day.” I slowly danced into the darkest corner of the room where no one would notice us.

"Look at my face, Noel. I'm like that Batman character, Two-Face. One side of the mirror is Savannah, but the other side of the mirror is someone I don't know."

I held her tighter to me and stopped moving my feet, just swaying her to look as though we were dancing when we were really just hugging.

"It's okay to be scared, Savannah."

"I'm trying not to be, but it gets harder every day. Thank you for everything you've done to help me this past week. I don't know what I would have done if you hadn't moved here, I know that for sure."

"I'm glad I listened to that inner voice telling me to move to Snowberry. I don't always understand the universe, but sometimes, you have to trust it."

"I don't understand any of this either," she said, motioning to her face. "I don't understand what I'm supposed to do or how I'm supposed to feel or act. I had no one in my life but Snow, and suddenly I have Dully and his whole family supporting me. I have sweet Sunny who makes me smile, even if only half my face will do it now. I have December who befriended me without knowing just how desperately I needed her, and now because of her, you're in my life. I don't know that I'll ever understand the universe."

"But you trust all of us to keep you safe, right?"

I asked.

She was quiet for several moments. "Yes, my heart knows none of you would ever hurt me. Snow and I have been through so much together. She has always been the leader in this friendship, and I've learned to follow her." She laughed a little, and I rubbed her back, enjoying the feel of her in my arms and the warmth of her against my chest.

"Then you don't have to understand why. You can just let us protect you. You don't have to suffer alone anymore. You've been strong and independent for so long, but sometimes you need to take a break. It doesn't mean you're weak. In fact, just the opposite is true. It means you've been strong too long. Let someone else carry the burdens for a while."

"You think so?" she asked, surprised. I nodded against her head. "That sounds nice, but my burdens remain my own. I still have this problem to figure out."

"I know, but you have all of us to help you do that now. That's all I'm saying."

The music died off, and the lights came up, so I led her off the floor and back to her chair. I sat next to her, never letting go of her hand. The DJ had the microphone, and after a few tries, he finally got everyone's attention. "It's time for the family dances. Will the groom and his mother and the bride and her father come to the floor?"

I cringed, and my eyes immediately locked with December's. Her feet were rooted to the floor next to Jay. Jay rolled his chair toward the DJ, but his dad, Tom, stopped him. He held out his hand to my sister, who gratefully accepted it with a smile on her face, even though you could tell she was shaken.

The music started and they danced to *You are the Sunshine of my Life*. Soon Dully cut in to dance with December for a few moments, and whispered words were said. Then he handed her over to his brother, Jake, who danced with her for a moment and handed her over to Dully. He spun her around the floor once and handed her off to their younger brother, Bram.

I stood up and patted Savannah's hand. "I'll be right back."

I tapped Bram on the shoulder. "May I cut in?" I asked gallantly, and he bowed, holding December's hand out.

I swooped her into me, and she smiled up at me, tears in her eyes. "They're wonderful," she whispered.

"I think so, too. I'm glad you have a whole bunch of brothers now to watch over you. It makes my job easier."

"Or frees you up to take care of someone else?" she asked, her eyes drifting to the table where Savannah sat with Sunny on her lap, and Snow keeping a close eye on them.

I laughed at her less than subtle hint. "That, too. I'm just glad I got you alone for a few moments."

She rested her head on my shoulder. "It has been busy, hasn't it?"

"Yes, but that's good. Look at all the people who love you here. It makes me feel a little better about the years I was a horse's behind to you. I hate myself for making you feel alone, but this town took care of you."

"Noel, we can't change the past, so don't hate yourself because of what happened. We promised a new start, which means no looking back," she ordered.

"You're right, I'm trying. Let me live in the past for just a few minutes tomorrow, and then I'll stop feeling bad about the last years and move forward," I promised.

"Tomorrow? What's going on tomorrow?" she asked, surprised.

"I was hoping to bring by a few things I brought with me from the house. Nick is living there now and taking care of the place for us, but there were some things I thought you might like to have. If tomorrow doesn't work, I can bring them over whenever," I added quickly. I didn't want her to change her plans if she and Jay were busy.

"We'll be home tomorrow afternoon. Neither of us has enough vacation for a honeymoon, so we're going to enjoy some short weekend trips over the next few months. We'd love to see you, but I would guess you better come after the game if you don't want to be hushed all afternoon long." She grinned, and I snickered.

"The Alexander boys do love their football. How about I come over about three?" She nodded her agreement and left her head on my shoulder as the rest of the song played out.

The DJ spoke into the microphone again. "If the gentleman would hand off the bride to her groom, it is time for their first dance."

I kissed December on the cheek and gave her hand to Jay, who shook mine, then pulled December onto his lap, her legs swung across his chair. *You are So Beautiful* began playing, and Jay held December on his lap while Sport drove them around the floor, spinning and turning to the beat of the music. I walked back to the table where Savannah and the rest of the family sat. Dully stood up from the chair next to Savannah, so I could sit.

I leaned over into Snow's ear. "Is that your handiwork?"

She snickered and whispered back, "Jay and I did a little tinkering with a program on a flash drive. So far, so good."

I smiled as they danced, December wholly lost in the moment of being in her husband's arms the way any other bride would be.

I lifted Savannah's hand off her lap and gave it a gentle squeeze. Her face was covered by her hair, but she squeezed my hand back. When the song ended, and everyone stood to clap, I laid my lips by her ear. "Trust me when I tell you this. You're the most beautiful woman in this room right now."

Chapter Six

Savannah

I stopped at the entrance of my dining room to watch the man in my kitchen. He was humming to himself as he cooked a late breakfast of eggs and bacon. When he found time to go shopping, I didn't know, but miraculously, my fridge was filled to almost overflowing with healthy food.

He was definitely in his element with his flannel shirt sleeves rolled to his elbows and untucked from his pair of Levi 501s. He certainly wasn't what most women would consider lumberjack material. He was more of a string bean with gorgeous hazel eyes and short hair, shaved short on the side.

His height and long limbs should have made him gangly and awkward, but instead, every movement he made was fluid and natural. Whether he was cooking, helping me tie flowers, or holding me on the dance floor, he exuded confidence. I closed my eyes and swallowed at the thought of us on the dance floor.

Last night was a lot of fun, and his insistence that I was beautiful gave me the confidence to step out of the house. Not that I had much choice in the matter. My business wasn't going to run itself, so hiding in the house wasn't an option, personally or professionally. His kindness in paying for the hairdo and buying the eye patches helped a lot, though. When most men wouldn't look twice at me, he couldn't take his eyes off me.

I'm woman enough to admit that it makes me feel a little bit better about myself. I have absolutely nothing to offer him right now, and if he still likes me, then he must be genuine, right? I sighed and my hand went to my eye patch, touching the soft material. When I opened my other eye, he was in front of me.

"Are you okay?" he asked tenderly.

I dropped my hand and nodded. "Yes, why?"

He took my hand and led me into the kitchen to sit on a barstool while he finished breakfast.

"I heard you moan and thought maybe the pain was back," he answered, flipping the bacon in the pan.

I spun a glass of juice he had put in front of me. "No, sorry, I was just thinking. Thank you, by the way, for last night. I'm glad you were here."

His shoulders drooped, and he flipped the eggs before he turned around. "You don't have to thank me, Savannah. I can't stand to see you in that kind of pain. It feels disproportionate to me, even with what you have going on. I really want you to see that specialist at Mayo."

We had a stare off for a few moments, and I

was the first to give in and glance away. After we got home last night, the fatigue of the previous few days caught up to me, and when my pajamas brushed over my face, it seized up. I fell against the door and he came running. He scooped me up onto the couch and held an icepack to my face until the attack subsided. It was so late by then that I fell asleep with the comfort of the ice dulling the pain. When I woke up this morning, he was sleeping on the floor next to me, his hand still resting on the couch.

"It scared me, too," I admitted. "The pain is getting worse, and now with this whole thing," I motioned at my eye, "I don't know what to do. How long did Snow think the medication would take to start helping?"

He took the bacon off the stove and drained it on a paper towel and then filled our plates with eggs, bacon, and toast, carrying both plates to the small bar. He took a bite of his eggs and the heat had him gulping his orange juice quickly.

"Noel?" I asked, surprised by his sudden uncomfortableness.

He set his glass down slowly. "Snow told me last night she didn't really expect the medication to work at all, it was just a last-ditch effort because she doesn't know how to help you. It's killing her."

I stared down at my plate of food. My stomach rolled and my eyes burned. I was a burden even to my best friend now, and I hated that more than I hated the way my face looked.

"She told me she offered to pay for the visit to the specialist, but you refused?" he questioned, while he chewed on a piece of bacon.

I didn't even bother to look up. "I don't want to be a burden to my friends, Noel. I'm an adult and I should have figured this out by now."

"How does letting your friend help make you a burden?"

I sighed and poked at the eggs with my fork. "If I see the specialist, he's going to say I need tests and probably surgery. I can't ask her to pay for all of that, it would bankrupt anyone. Why bother going? It's like being hungry and going to a restaurant and reading the menu, but knowing you can't actually order anything."

He took another bite of eggs and chewed slowly. "I guess I can see your point."

I took a forkful of eggs even though I wasn't that hungry. They were fluffier than any egg I had ever eaten in my life. "How do you do that?" I asked, motioning to the eggs.

He grinned and shook his head. "I can't tell you. It's a family secret, and you're not family yet."

"Yet?" I asked, surprised.

He set his fork down and came around the bar, taking my hand. Without a word, he led me into the living room and sat down on the couch with me.

"I didn't get much sleep last night, Savannah," he started.

"I'm sorry. I know, that was my fault," I apologized.

"No, angel, stop apologizing, please. Besides, you were sleeping peacefully. This had nothing to do with you and everything to do with you."

"What are you talking about, Noel Kiss? I think you've lost your mind," I joked, checking his forehead for a fever.

"Sometimes, I don't disagree with you. The last month has been a bit crazy. I've never thrown caution to the wind when it comes to my business. I always plot out all the possible pros and cons of opening a café in a specific location before I even consider looking for a property. I do the math ten times and then do it again, just to be sure. I check demographics and distance to the closest highways and interstate. That's what a businessman does, but this time I did none of that. I drove into a town I had only been in twice and made business decisions without a second thought. I didn't have to think because I knew I was doing the right thing. Does that make sense?"

"The decisions were easy to make because your heart told you they were the right ones," I answered, and he nodded.

"Exactly. Well, last night, I was watching you sleep and it was kind of the same thing," he admitted, holding my hand.

"I don't follow."

"That's okay. I can't say that I do, either. After you fell asleep, I knew I should go to my room, but I didn't want to leave you alone. I started thinking about what I could do to help you with your problem."

I waved my hand so he would stop talking. "Noel, my problem isn't your responsibility to solve."

"I know, but after witnessing the last few attacks you've had, I'm just incredibly worried about you. I'm afraid if you don't go see the specialist that you'll have to live in this kind of pain forever."

I stared at him wide-eyed and nodded slowly. "I think about that a lot, too."

"My mom died of an aortic aneurysm that she didn't even know she had. It turns out her doctor had mentioned several times that he wanted to investigate her high blood pressure further, but she refused. She said she didn't have time and just give her more pills. She died because of that decision," he explained sadly.

I held his hand, and his pain and guilt were palpable in the room, even after all these years. "I'm sorry if living here is making you uncomfortable. I understand if you want to move out."

He glanced up instantly and shook his head. "No, I don't want to move out, angel. I don't think I'm explaining this very well." He sighed and rubbed his forehead a few times. "I don't want to move out, but I also don't want to regret not taking action. After hours of plotting out ideas and making pros and cons lists, I only found one solution."

"You did? What is it? If you have an answer to this, I'm all ears."

"We have to get married," he said calmly and evenly.

I dropped his hand and sat back against the couch. "Excuse me?"

"Sorry for the blunt delivery, but it's the only answer that makes sense." He stared at me intently, waiting for my reaction.

"You think that marrying me is the right answer?" I asked, confused.

"I know it sounds ridiculous." He rolled his eyes a little bit and shook his head.

"I don't know about ridiculous, but maybe a little farfetched." I gave him the palms up, trying to let him down easy.

"Fair enough, but hear me out. I'm living with you already, so not that farfetched. If we get married, I can put you on my health insurance plan. Once you're on my insurance, you can finally see the specialist. You can have all the testing and surgery you need, and we won't have to worry about the cost," he finished, running his hands on his pants.

"Noel, you're telling me you want to marry me, so I can have insurance, which you will pay for, to treat an injury resulting from another man?"

He grimaced. "It would be easier if you didn't put it that way."

"You have to forgive me. I'm surprised and trying to process all of this quickly. I wasn't trying to put it any certain way. I was just trying to make sense of it. Is that even legal?" I asked, and he nodded.

“As long as we’re married and living together, it’s legal. We already have the living together part done,” he pointed out, and it was my turn to rub my forehead.

“Be that as it may, it’s wrong. I think that’s called insurance fraud.”

He leaned back against his side of the couch, too. “I know and that’s what I fought with most of the night. It was in my sleep that I finally decided it was the right thing to do. In a dream, actually.”

“I’m a little afraid to ask.” I laughed, and he squeezed my thigh gently in support.

“It’s okay. I turned the water on cold full blast in the shower this morning just to make sure I was actually awake. The word crazy has come to mind a few times in the last six hours. In this dream, I was interviewing people to work at my café. The only person who came to the interview was Snow.”

“Snow, a research doctor, came to an interview at your café?”

“Surprising, I know. I think it was more symbolic than anything, though.”

“I see. Forgive me for interrupting.”

“Yeah, so anyway. You know what, forget I said anything. Saying it out loud really makes me sound crazy. You don’t know me well enough to know that I’m not crazy and you might decide I can’t live here. Hell, I don’t even know if I’m sane anymore.” He blew out a puff of breath and ran his hands through his hair.

I laid my hand on his arm. “I don’t think you’re crazy, and I don’t want you to move out. I do want you to tell me the rest of the dream.”

He squinted at me nervously. “Are you sure?” I nodded and he picked up my hand and drew a pattern across my palm. “Okay, well, in the dream, I sat at the table, staring at Snow, who sat across from me. She was free of the chair and absolutely stunning as the sun shone through her white hair. I was supposed to interview her, but I couldn’t speak. She spoke first and said, ‘What if you marry her?’ It was only after she asked me the question that I could speak again. I said, ‘What if she says no?’ Her response was, ‘What if she says yes?’”

I studied him without saying anything while he rubbed my palm absently.

“You’re telling me that Snow came to you in a dream and told you to marry me.”

“Trust me, I thought it was as weird as you do right now. I still wasn’t sure what she was getting at, so she asked me to sit quietly and think about the different ways history would be changed depending upon your answer.”

I raised a brow. “That’s heavy stuff.”

“It is. I could see a lot of different ways it could go. If I don’t help you get the treatment you need, and that breaks a chain, how does that change the history of Snowberry or your family? What if I don’t marry you and you don’t get help. What if you never have the child that was supposed to cure cancer because you couldn’t live through the pain?

How does that change the history of mankind?"

I paused and thought about what he was saying for a few moments. "The possibilities are endless there, Noel."

He picked up my hand to stop my fidgeting. "They are, and I woke up thinking the same thing. I'm sure it was subliminal messaging from my mind because I'd been thinking about it before I fell asleep. In the end, I decided it was another message."

"What was the message? That you're supposed to ask and see what I say?"

He shook his head slowly. "No, I'm supposed to do anything in my power to help you, even if everyone around us thinks it's radical."

I sat quietly for the longest time, trying to digest what he was saying. "If we get married, I can go to the specialist and get treatment, but then what? Do we just get divorced?"

He laughed a little and held up his palms. "I guess we can work that out after we know you're healed and healthy."

I rubbed the tape around my eye patch and looked up at him, "We have to concentrate on the present and not worry about the future?"

He nodded. "The present might sort the future out. If we trust each other, we can do anything."

I stared at our hands linked together and then made eye contact with him. "Trust each other?" he nodded and I blew out a breath. "If you're certain this will work, then maybe we should do it."

"I have no lingering doubts, but I want you to be comfortable, too. I don't want to push you into doing something you don't want to do."

He ran the back of his hand down my cheek and I closed my eyes, loving the way it felt to be cared for by a man who I knew would never hurt me.

When my eyes opened, I glanced down at the couch. Holding his honest ones was too much for me when I had to admit the truth. "I'm not comfortable right now. My whole head hurts so much that I never get a break from it. I don't know how much longer I can take it, Noel." There were tears in my eyes and he tilted my chin up. There were tears in his eyes, too.

"I know, that's why I'm desperate to help you, angel. I can't even imagine what you're going through."

I swallowed hard and nodded. "I know that what you're proposing will help me find a solution to the pain, so I think we need to do this."

He rested his hand behind my neck comfortingly. "I want to make your pain go away. That's all I want."

"How are we going to pull this off, Noel? We're going to pretend to be madly in love and we've never even kissed."

"We can fix that," he promised, lowering his head to mine.

I braced my hand on his chest. "Noel, I can't kiss you."

He pulled back and dropped his hand from my back. "I'm sorry I didn't mean to make you feel uncomfortable."

I ran my finger down his cheek and smiled. "I'm not uncomfortable. I just mean I can't." I motioned at my face and rolled my eye a little.

He grasped my hand and leaned in, laying his lips against mine for just a moment before he pulled away. "Let me do the work."

In a breath, his lips were back on mine, and he kissed me in a way I'd never been kissed before. His lips were demanding, but gentle, and even though I couldn't make my lips do what I wanted, I tried to return the kiss with as much thankfulness as I could. The problem was, I was feeling everything but thankful. I was feeling things from his kiss I had never felt even from my husband. His lips warmed mine and I felt safe, yet sexy and desired, at the same time.

I wound my arms around his neck and he scooted closer, pulling me onto his lap. Slowly, his lips left mine, and he kissed my left cheek then pulled me into a hug, being careful of my face.

"I like how you feel in my arms," he admitted, loosening his hold a little, "but you don't have to worry, my brain knows this marriage is a sham. I'm not going to hold you to any marital duties."

He laid a kiss on my forehead gently, and I fought against telling him that some marital duties I wouldn't mind being held to.

Chapter Seven

Noel

I dropped Savannah off at the shop at opening time and wandered next door to the café. The crew wasn't working, of course, since it was Sunday, so I let myself in the front door and stood in the middle of the mess that was my business. The old tables, chairs, and carpet were gone, leaving a sanded wood floor that, with a little bit of coating would glisten in the lights of the new café. I reached down and touched the smooth wood and my mind instantly went to the smooth feel of her lips on mine.

I still couldn't believe she agreed to marry me, even though the whole idea was looney tunes. Then again, pain and desperation made a person do things they otherwise might not. The trick would be convincing other people we were in love, and that it wasn't a marriage of convenience. We decided it was best to let people think we were in love, including our families.

When I asked her why she didn't have insurance, she told me she simply couldn't afford the almost eight hundred dollars a month for the premium. That was for a policy that covered nothing more than doctor visits. If she wanted coverage for surgical care or emergency care, it went up from there.

I leaned against the wall and stared out over the empty dining room. Insurance wasn't exactly affordable for anyone, especially those of us who run small businesses. I knew that firsthand. Fortunately, I now have enough cafes that, if we all have the same plan, we get good coverage at an affordable price. If I could have figured out a way to put her on the payroll, I would have, but since she owns her own business, there was no way to do that either.

After kissing her today, I knew one thing for sure, she might be marrying me for my insurance, but I hoped if I worked hard, and treated her right, she wouldn't want a divorce once she was healed. It didn't take me any time to realize I moved to Snowberry for one reason and one reason only. Savannah Hart. I only had a few months to show her a lifetime of love or I might lose her forever. I had to show her she deserves love and happiness in life. Right now, she believes she's getting what she deserves. The whole idea set my teeth on edge and I was going to prove her otherwise.

I was so lost in thought I jumped at the loud knocking. I glanced up, and April was waving at me through the newly installed picture window. I pushed off the wall and motioned for her to come in. She pulled the door open and stopped in the middle of the room, turning around in a slow three-sixty.

"It looks so different," she said. "Everyone is going to love it."

It took me a few moments to decipher what she said, but when I did, I smiled. "I hope so. There will be booths on the wall there and there." I pointed toward the picture window and the wall behind it. "A low counter here where you can sit and eat while watching the cook, and the back wall will have bigger tables for larger groups. There will be two lowered tables for wheelchair users, and that spot right there." I pointed to the left of the kitchen, and she nodded. "That's going to be the hallway to the front door. The back will be the main entrance and parking lot. It's safer than having families parking on the street with their little ones and crossing. It also gives me ample room to put in a nice handicapped accessible ramp, without infringing on the sidewalk."

She nodded her approval. "It sounds well planned out. How long until it's finished?"

"Big Eddie told me I should be able to open by the middle of February. They're really moving on the place, and since the kitchen is done, it's really only a matter of getting the back door installed, the ramp built, and the interior finished."

She chuckled. "If Big Eddie is on the job, you'll be open long before the middle of February. This type of eatery is his favorite place to be. He's chomping at the bit to get you open, so he can have his Friday fish fry and his Sunday morning pancakes again."

I joined her in her laughter. "You mean offering him, and his crew, free pancakes every Sunday for getting this job done was a mistake?"

She full out giggled at that remark. "A mistake you will never make again. I can promise you that."

"What brings you by, April?" I asked, flipping over a couple of five-gallon buckets so we could sit.

"Oh, well, after Savannah got sick the other day and everything, I didn't get a chance to talk to you again. I have the hiring information for you and I was going to email it, but I don't have your email," she explained shyly.

I smacked my forehead. "Of course, that's right. Sorry about that, I was worried about Savannah and forgot all about it."

"I understand. She isn't in good shape right now. She really needs to see a doctor."

"She does, and she's going to as soon as she can get an appointment at Mayo. She's a little stubborn, but she can't hold a candle to my level of stubbornness."

She leaned forward and gave me a high five. "Good. I might be young, but I know the importance of not letting something like that go just because you don't want to miss work. I'm more than happy to run the emporium when she's gone. I'll even do it for free if it means she doesn't have to worry about it and gets to feeling better."

I sat back on the bucket in surprise. "Really?

You would work the emporium for nothing?"

"Savannah would do it for anyone else who needed help. She's always sending flowers to the nursing home and to people in the hospital who don't have any family. She donates flowers for prom and then makes sure they get to the nursing home the next day for the senior prom they hold every year. She's known around here as the smile maker."

I could tell it was the truth because she was grinning ear-to-ear. "Well, now, you learn something new every day." I pondered. "You know what, April? I might just need someone like you on my team. What's your background? Retail or something else?"

"Actually, I have a degree in accounting and bookkeeping. I've worked some odd jobs at shops like Savannah's, but usually just as favors. My real love is the numbers game," she admitted, pulling her hair down around her cheeks.

"A degree in accounting, you say? I could use someone with that kind of experience. I need somewhat of a personal assistant until the place is up and running, and then you could transfer to doing the books. Do you have any management experience?" I asked, grabbing my phone from my pocket.

"Not in a restaurant atmosphere. I used to manage the gift shop at the hospital when I was a volunteer there, but that's about the extent of it. I'm not comfortable dealing with a lot of people all at once," she admitted uncomfortably.

"You don't like being overwhelmed? I can understand that. Restaurant work can be overwhelming."

She stared down at the floor for a moment then back to my face. "Not so much that, but I have to read lips and I would hate to have someone order one thing and get something else because I put the order in wrong. I wouldn't make a good waitress or anything," she said with honesty.

This girl was full of surprises. "I see," I said slowly. "I cannot legally ask you why you read lips."

"No, but I can tell you. I'm completely deaf. It doesn't stop me from working, though. I like Savannah's because it never gets hectic and..."

She was talking so fast I couldn't understand what she was saying. "Slow down, April. It's okay, you don't have to explain. We all have our strengths and weaknesses. I can make a mean omelet and peel over two hundred potatoes an hour with my trusty drill, but I can't carry a tray of food to a table to save my soul, at least not without dumping it. I'm all about finding the right people to fill the right positions, not just fill the positions."

She settled a bit and folded her hands. "I'm glad you understand."

"Absolutely, so are you interested in a position where you start out with helping me get the café open and then transition into the bookwork and manager type work?" I asked.

"Yes, sir, very much so," she answered honestly.

"Good, one thing, though. No more *sir*, it makes me feel ancient. Just call me Noel."

"Of course, sorry. I'm suddenly nervous. I wasn't prepared for an interview today," she conceded and then pulled her phone from her pocket.

"No need to be nervous at all. I'm easy to get along with, and I appreciate how willing you are to jump into the fray here and get things going. Since the café won't be open for another month, would you be willing to run the emporium for Savannah when I take her to Mayo? She might need someone for a week or two, but she would only be a phone call away. I would be paying you, so you won't be working for free," I explained, and she nodded along.

"I would be happy to. When it's quiet at the emporium, I can work on reading résumés and setting up interviews. It's really no problem. It gives me a place to work and helps out Savannah at the same time."

"Perfect, actually, wait. I have to ask a question. It won't keep me from hiring you, but I do need to know if adjustments need to be made in how we do things."

I saw the recognition in her eyes then. "Oh, you mean my hearing or lack thereof. Go ahead and ask, I don't mind."

"I was just wondering about the phone system. How will you set up interviews and contact companies?"

"That's a legitimate question. You can hear my voice is different than most, but I learned to speak before I became deaf. To answer your question, I would hold an interview day where people can come and interview on the spot. I'll be honest, they work far better than the traditional way of putting in an application and then trying to get through to them to set up an interview. In this day and age, everyone, and I mean even Grandpa Frank, has a cell phone. We will be doing a lot of emailing, all saved, of course. Personally, I think it's better for the employer and the employee when the conversations are written. There's no *he said she said* case then." She paused and I thought it over, finally conceding she had a point. "I assume you'll have internet and a phone line in the office once the café is open?" she asked.

"Yes, of course, not for customer use, though. I want people to come in to eat and talk to each other."

She pointed at me. "I like that, that's not done enough nowadays. Anyway, as long as you have those two things, then I have a special phone I can bring in. Anyone who calls in will have their calls captioned for me to read. It's a free service, and whether I'm calling out or someone is calling in, I can get the captions I need. Is that acceptable?" she asked professionally and I had to hand it to her, she didn't let anything stop her.

"More than acceptable, except, please, let me

get the phones and have them installed. I assume they can also be used without the captioning system, so say I can have one upfront for call-in orders, etc.?" I asked, making notes on my phone.

"Oh, yes, if you want the captions, you just push the button. That would be fine if you want to get the phones, they are usually minimally more expensive than a regular phone if you get them from the phone company," she informed me, and then gave me the name of the phone and the type that worked with the internet.

"I learned something new today, April. I appreciate that you are open and willing to be honest about what you need. I want to make your job as easy as possible, and this is certainly no problem. I agree with you about the interview hiring day, too. I had nothing but trouble trying to hire new employees until I went to that kind of venue. Now, I won't do it any other way when I'm trying to fill all the positions for a new café. We're on the same wavelength, and that's great. All we have to decide on is your wage and when you want to start. For now, since we don't have an open business, I'll pay you twenty bucks an hour until the business opens and then I'll pay you manager's salary with full benefits?" I asked, trying to get a feel for what she thought was fair.

Her eyes were wide. "Really? That would be very acceptable, Noel. I appreciate your confidence in me."

"And I appreciate your willingness to have an

interview on a five-gallon bucket in an empty café." I laughed, and she did, too.

"Hey, some of the best ideas are hatched this way." She opened her phone and pulled up her notes. "Let me show you the information I have so far, and you can tell me what you'd like me to concentrate on this week."

I moved my bucket closer, so I could see the screen, and once again thanked the universe for putting the right person in my path at the right time.

I had a beautiful woman who smelled like gardenias in my truck, and a large pizza pie from Gallo's that smelled like pepperoni. They both made me hungry, just in different ways.

When I called December and asked if we could come at five, when Savannah closed the shop, she had no problem with it, especially after I offered to bring Gallo's.

"You look nervous, Savannah," I shared, kissing her hand that I held on my lap.

"I'm a little nervous. I've never pretended to be in love before. On top of it, it's your family," she pointed out.

"December might be my family by blood, but they were your family long before they were mine. They love you and want you to be happy. All I can do is hope they trust me to do that."

"You're saying you don't have the best track record?" She laughed and I shook my head.

"Not if you take into account the last eight years. I mean, at least not with my family. I see that now. I hope that being in Snowberry means December and I can get back to being twins. I mean, we are twins, but to understand each other on the level like we used to as twins. I'm making no sense." I clamped my lips shut.

She pulled her hand from mine and rubbed my shoulder. "Yes, you are. You know you can't make up for what happened the last eight years, but if you show her how much you love her, things will get back to the way they used to be and you can be a family again."

"You get me, that's for sure." I smiled and turned into Snow's driveway. "As for being nervous about pretending to be in love." I shrugged. "Don't pretend, just act natural and the rest will come to you. That's what I'm going to do."

I put the truck in park behind Jay's truck and caught the look she gave me out of the corner of her eye. It was a look of confusion and then realization, but I was out of the truck before she had a chance to say anything. I came around the side and helped her down, taking the pizza from her. I balanced it on one arm while I held her hand and helped her down the path. I would come back up later for the items I brought for December.

"You know we're going to have to talk to Snow

about this," she pointed out on our trip down to Jay's cabin.

"She's the one we really have to convince. I don't want to put her in a tough position because we're using this marriage as a way to get you insurance."

She stopped walking and looked up at me. "You're kidding me, right? You've met Snow, no? Right now, she'd make a deal with the devil if it meant I went to the doctor."

I shook my finger at her and grinned. "You make a point there, but I'd still rather she thinks the same as everyone else."

"You want me to lie to my best friend."

It wasn't a question but a statement.

I was about to say yes when I closed my mouth and took a moment to think. I ran my free hand down the left side of her face and tucked in a stray lock of her golden-brown hair.

"I don't want you to do anything you aren't comfortable doing. If telling Snow you're in love with me, and that's why we're getting married, makes you uncomfortable then tell her the truth. She might see right through us anyway, but I know, either way, she'll be happy you're going to get treatment," I whispered.

"Hey, are you two coming in here before that pizza is a popsicle?" my sister yelled from the door of the cabin.

Savannah bit back a snort, and I grabbed her hand again to finish the walk up the ramp.

"The pizza won't get cold, it's already nice and warm, in my belly!" I yelled back, and now Savannah was holding her face and laughing behind her hand.

"Don't lie to me, little brother, I can smell the pepperoni from here," she called.

We walked the remaining twenty feet to the cottage door. "Little brother by three minutes," I scoffed.

December held the door open for Savannah and then stopped me with her hand on my chest. "And don't you forget it."

I grinned and kissed her on the cheek, handing her the pizza box as promised. I took Savannah's coat and hung it, and mine, on the coat tree near the door. The cabin was warm, with a fire crackling in the fireplace. I always got a feeling of warmth and acceptance when I was in the cabin.

"Hi, Jay, thanks for letting us barge in on you tonight," I said, shaking his hand from where he sat on the couch.

"My door is always open to family. You aren't barging in at all. Glad you could make it, actually. I know we haven't had much time to get to know each other." Jay accepted a beer and a plate of pizza from December and then pulled her down for a kiss.

"It has been pretty crazy since Christmas, but you two are settling in well." I took a plate from December, and Savannah sat on the couch next to me. I wanted to say she was relaxed, but I could feel the tension radiating from her.

December flopped down in the big chair next to Jay and threw her legs over the arm. "Pretty crazy? It's been nuts. Now, I find out that my little brother is moving to town and opening a café. It's hard to keep up."

I set my plate down and squeezed Savannah's hand for support. "Then we might as well tell you right now, so we're all on the same page. Savannah and I are getting married."

Jay stopped with his pizza halfway to his mouth, and December's eyes flicked back and forth between Savannah and me. The sound of silence was deafening.

December leaned forward. "A few days ago, you were moving in and *just friends*." She put it in air quotes and I swallowed hard. "Now, you're getting married?"

"I, uh, I hadn't asked her yet and I didn't want to jinx it," I stuttered, taking Savannah's hand and kissing it. Acting cool wasn't working under my sister's pointed stare.

Jay sat forward and stuck his hand out. "Congratulations, Noel. I'm not one to question falling in love with someone at first sight." He glanced at December and grinned. "But you better be good to her."

I shook his hand and nodded my head along with each pump. "Thanks, Jay. Don't worry, I love her, and that makes it awfully easy to be good to her."

December stood slowly and came over to us, kneeling down in front of me. "You took me by surprise, but I'm happy for both of you. Everyone can see how much you love each other."

She hugged me then, and I wrapped my arms around her back, surprised by her declaration. This was a fake marriage. There was no love, right? Savannah stood quickly and almost tripped over December.

"I need to use the bathroom," she said, and Jay pointed down the hall.

"Second door on the right."

"Is she okay?" December asked, and I wondered the same thing myself.

"Give her a few minutes and I'll check on her," I answered, hoping she was just trying to regain her composure.

"She's not wearing a ring," my sister pointed out, sitting back down in her chair.

"It's at the jewelers," I lied. Well, it wasn't actually a lie. There are rings at the jeweler. All I got from her was one eyebrow raised.

"Seems like I heard this story before."

Jay laughed and I tried not to drop my eyes from December's. Last month, when she came to my café and told me she was getting married, I called her on the fact she wasn't wearing a ring. It looked like she was returning the favor.

"It's not a story. There are lots of rings at the jeweler. I'm taking her tomorrow to pick out a set with me. I want to make sure she gets something she wants, and that works with what she does for a living," I explained.

Jay chuckled. "Did you have a little too much to drink last night and pop the question unexpectedly, Noel?"

I wasn't amused. "No, I was stone-cold sober, as a matter of fact. Maybe I didn't do things in the right order, but my heart was in the right place."

Jay threw his hands up in defense. "I was just joking around, Noel. I apologize. It's none of our business how or why you asked her to marry you."

Jay tried to soothe me, but I was suddenly anxious. December kept looking toward the hallway, too.

"I think I hear crying."

I was down the hallway before she finished. I knocked on the door and called to her, but got no answer. The handle turned in my hand and I pushed the door open carefully to find her holding her face over the sink.

"I'm here, sweetheart. Let me help you," I soothed. I scooped her up and carried her out of the bathroom. "December, get an icepack," I yelled from the hallway as I carried her into the spare bedroom and laid her down on the bed. Her face was contorted, the muscles spasming so tight it pulled her lips into an eerie Joker smile.

She gazed at me with her good eye, and the fear and pain in it made my heart rip apart in my chest. "I'm not going to leave you, just try to relax," I whispered, holding her hand.

December ran in with a towel wrapped pack and handed it to me. I held it to her face, the initial shock making Savannah cry out, but then she settled down as the numbing ice tricked the spasm into relaxing. December grabbed an afghan from the closet and laid it over Savannah, fussing over her like only a nurse can. She took her pulse and did a quick assessment, even if Savannah was too out of it to know she was doing it.

"Her heart is racing," she whispered, glancing up at me.

"The spasm is ending now. She'll be worn out and fall asleep for a bit, then it will go back to normal," I explained. She patted my shoulder and pointed to the living room and I nodded.

Savannah tried to speak, but I hushed her. "Don't talk honey, just rest. You have to relax if you want the pain to go away. I know that's hard, but just close your eyes and think about spring at Snowberry Lake. We can walk along the paths and watch the little kids fishing from the piers, then stop and have a picnic on a little patch of grass under a tree."

I kept talking to her, planning out an afternoon at the lake until her breathing was soft and even. The pain in my heart loosened a little bit and I pulled the blanket up closer to her chin without disturbing the icepack. She would sleep now and hopefully wake up feeling a little bit better, but she would likely be utterly embarrassed that it happened here. I waited until her hand relaxed and fell from mine before I went back to the front room where the pizza was long forgotten and Jay was holding December on the couch.

December sat up when she saw me. "How is she?"

"She's asleep. The attacks always wear her out, and she has to sleep for a bit to get her strength back."

"Are they getting worse? Last night at the dance, Snow told me she gave her prednisone," December said and uncurled herself from Jay.

"They're getting worse, and more frequent since her face became paralyzed like that. Snow was trying the prednisone to see if it would give her movement back in her face, but it hasn't made any difference," I explained.

There was a rush of cold air on my back, and I turned to see Snow wheeling through the front door, not even wearing a coat.

"Where is she?" she asked, without stopping the chair.

I grabbed it as she passed me. "She's sleeping now, Snow. She'll be awake in a few minutes," I assured her.

She ran her hands through her hair, "Why does she have to be so stubborn? She has to see a doctor. She just has to."

I nodded in agreement. "I finally convinced her of the same. We were going to stop at your house on our way out, but since you're here, I'll tell you. If you can get her an appointment with the doctor at

Mayo, I'll make sure she gets there."

She dropped her hands to her rounded belly. "She has an appointment. I called on Friday. She needs to be there Wednesday at ten. Dr. Kent is going to see her as a professional courtesy. I'll figure out how to pay for surgery if that arises. I was going to ask December to watch the emporium and drive her down there myself."

Relief flowed through me like I hadn't felt in a very long time. I didn't take a lot of time to analyze it before I patted Snow's shoulder. "I just hired April Melody as my personal assistant. She'll be available to keep the flower shop open when Savannah needs time off. Eventually, April will be my manager and bookkeeper at the café, but for now, she's pulling double duty."

Snow stared at me for a long time. "You really care about Savannah, don't you?"

I took her hand off her belly and hoped whatever emotions she saw in my eyes would match my words. "I love Savannah, so much so I'm going to marry her. You won't have to worry about anything. I'll make sure she gets the treatment she needs."

"What? You're going to marry her? Whoa, slow down. I'm getting whiplash," she whispered.

December giggled softly. "So were we, but he loves her, and he asked her to marry him."

Snow got a suspicious look in her eyes. "When?"

"Last night," I gulped.

"What did she say?"

"Yes," I squeaked.

"Just like that?" she questioned, one brow going up.

I could feel the sweat beading on my forehead. "Yes, just like that."

"You've only known her a few weeks. How do you know this is love?"

I knew the answer to this one and I let out a relieved breath. "My heart led me to Snowberry for a reason. My reason is Savannah, all beautiful five stubborn feet of her. I'll do whatever I have to do to end this pain for her and give her a life that makes her happy. I can't promise more than that."

Snow's shoulders slumped, and she swiped at a tear. "I'm so relieved. I can't even begin to tell you. I've been praying that you two would see how perfect you are for each other. She needs someone like you, Noel." She rolled her chair closer to me and grasped my shirt, pulling me down to eye level with her. "But I swear in front of everyone in this room, if you hurt her, I will kill you without a second thought."

I didn't laugh, look away, or do anything other than nod once. "Understood, and respected."

She released me, and I glanced around the room at the three people staring at me intently. "I don't want any of you to worry. I won't so much as burn her pancakes. She deserves to be treated like the wonderful, caring, sweet, giving woman that she is and I plan to do that. I also promise to make sure she gets the treatment she needs to repair her face and her heart."

"Can you afford that? It could be costly if she needs surgery, and I'm pretty sure she's going to," Snow fretted.

"I have insurance that will pay for the majority of it. I want you to stop worrying about this now. You've taken good care of her and made sure she got an appointment with the best doctor for her condition." I rested my hand on her tiny baby bump. "I don't want anything to happen to this little guy because you were stressed out."

She smiled and laid her hand over mine. "Little gal. We found out Friday we're having another girl."

I leaned in and gave her a kiss on the cheek. "Lucky little girl to have you as a mommy and little Sunny as a sister."

"You're not kidding," Jay spoke up. "Sunny didn't want anything to do with living with a boy. At least not one who couldn't drive her to get ice cream."

We all laughed and it was good to release the tension in the room. Maybe I'd fit in and be part of this family after all.

"When are you getting married?" Snow asked, readjusting herself in the chair.

"We'll get the license taken care of tomorrow, and we can get married on Saturday if that's okay with you. I know she'll want you to be a witness." I turned to Jay and December. "I was hoping you two would be mine."

"Absolutely, brother," Jay agreed.

"You don't want to wait and have a big wedding?" Snow asked slowly.

"I really want the ink dry sooner rather than later, so we can get her treatment. If, in the spring, she wants a big ceremony with all the pomp and circumstance, we will, but for now, I just need to make her mine. She did the big wedding once already, and wanted a private ceremony with just you, Dully, Sunny, Jay and December. She's a little self-conscious right now with everything." I motioned at my face and she nodded.

Snow put her hands on her wheels. "Maybe you know her better than I thought. I'm going to go check on her and take her vitals. I can't wait any longer."

I grabbed the wheel of her chair before she could leave. "That's fine, but don't let on that you know about the marriage, please? I know she really wanted to tell her bestie herself and I don't want to take that away from her. When she does tell you, would you act happy and upbeat? She tends to get the attacks when she's stressed out. Two in a row might land her in the ER." I didn't even care that I was pleading with this woman in front of my family.

She slipped her hand down over mine on the wheel. "I am happy, Noel. I won't be acting."

I gave her a relieved nod and she wheeled from the room.

Chapter Eight

The drive to Rochester was quiet and the sky was getting dusky as we pulled out of Snowberry. Yesterday, we filed for a marriage license at city hall. Savannah was nervous but accepted everyone's congratulations without having a facial spasm, so it was a good day.

At least she acted less stressed about pretending to love a man she barely knew. As soon as it was filed, I called the insurance company and added her to my policy, promising to fax the signed marriage license on Saturday. That meant she would be covered starting Monday and I was never more relieved to hear that. She wouldn't have to wait for any tests or surgery she may need.

I glanced over at her in the passenger seat of her car, her head resting on the seat while she slept. Sunday night, Snow gave her muscle relaxers in hopes that it would keep the spasms from being quite as painful. It might be working. Yesterday, she had an attack at the end of the day, but it wasn't as intense. The only downside was they made her sleepy and that drove her crazy. I made her promise to keep taking them until we saw the doctor tomorrow.

I spent the last two days working with April on setting up a job fair. There was plenty of trained staff available in town to work in the restaurant, and I told April we would give preference to any of Buck's employees who had a good track record with attendance and hadn't found another job already.

April took over the emporium for Savannah this afternoon, so we could head to Rochester tonight, instead of tomorrow morning. I hoped if she didn't feel rushed tomorrow, it would keep her from having an attack before she saw the doctor. You can't touch her face for hours after one and it would be torture if she had to see the doctor when it was tender.

She fell asleep when we were a few miles out of Snowberry, the medication taking its toll after working all day. I wrapped her up in a warm blanket and told her to relax while I drove. It was peaceful in the car and it left me alone with my thoughts for the first time in days. My eyes kept drifting to her face. She looked calm and peaceful, but I was looking at the left side of her face. I knew the other side was anything but calm and quiet, sort of the way her heart and mind were, too.

I hoped tomorrow after her appointment, she would feel up to stopping at the jewelry store to pick out a wedding band. She insists she doesn't want me to spend money on a ring and we could use a cheap one from any store. She said no one would be the wiser.

It took some convincing, but I finally talked her into a decent ring, not too expensive, but something people would believe was for life. I told her she couldn't wear a ring that left a green circle on her finger if it got wet. That got a laugh out of her and she finally agreed to something nice, but not too expensive. That did seem to be her hang up. She didn't want me wasting my money on her. Her words, not mine. My only response was that I don't waste money. I spend money on who and what I love. She didn't have an argument for that, which told me maybe I was slowly breaking down her defenses.

Something told me she hasn't had a lot of beautiful things in life. At least not given to her by someone else. I don't know her family story, but she obviously doesn't have family around to support her. The only pictures in her house are of Snow and her, and now Snow's family. I haven't asked about her family, because I'm worried it will bring on another attack. If she doesn't want to talk about it, I don't want to push it.

I turned off Highway 14 toward my house and the slowing of the car roused her from her sleep. "Where are we?" she asked groggily.

I laid my hand on her lap. "We're almost to my house. I let you sleep, so maybe you'd feel like having some dinner with me once we get settled in."

She stretched a little and her eyes strayed to the clock. "Man, it's so dark for it only being five-thirty. I am kind of hungry. How far is it to your house?"

I pointed out the windshield. "T minus four seconds." I grinned as she peered through the windshield.

"You live there? It's huge!" she exclaimed, sitting back abruptly.

"Nope, I don't live there. I live in this cute little bungalow with the best view." I winked and she fought a smile. "But this was my parents' house when we were kids. My dad had it paid off by the time he passed away, so my mom kept it. After she died, I couldn't part with it, so I paid December for her half and kept it. It's really only three bedrooms because my father turned one into a home office. I know I should sell it, but I will worry about that in the spring. For now, Nick is staying here and taking care of it."

I put the car in park and climbed out, going around to the passenger side and helping her out. I grabbed our duffel bags from the back and helped her up the driveway with my arm around her waist. Nick had the house open with lights glowing in the front room. I hung her coat up in the hall closet and then mine, waiting for the feeling of home to come over me. I waited, but it never happened. Now, it felt like my parents' house. The place where I was raised, but not the place that comforted me. It was strange and I shook it off.

"I need to use the bathroom," she said uncomfortably.

"Is it your face?" I asked instantly, but she shook her head.

"No, it's my bladder." She giggled, and I dropped my head into my hand.

"Sorry, let me show you."

I grinned sheepishly and took her hand, leading her down the hallway to the small powder room off the kitchen. "I'll be in the kitchen when you're done."

She nodded and closed the door. I wandered into the kitchen following the scent of roasted chicken. When I decided to drive down tonight, I asked Nick to whip up a couple of my favorite dishes and have them ready for me to heat up.

I found a note on the cupboard from him. *Dinner is on keep warm in the oven. Don't worry, if you're late the timer shuts it off after two hours. I know how you freak out about the house burning down." I started to laugh as I read. He was a great friend, but he was also a smart aleck. "There's dessert in the fridge and a bottle of wine in the cooler. I set the table on the porch in case you want a view with dinner. I'm working the nightshift. See you in the morning. Nick.*

I set the note down on the counter and opened the fridge. There was molten lava cake and I pulled it out, popping that in the oven to warm, and peeking at the roasted chicken and vegetables he had waiting for us.

"I feel incredibly inadequate," she whispered in awe when she found me in the kitchen.

"How come, angel?" I asked, taking her hand

and rubbing my thumb over the back of it.

"I just got lost trying to find the kitchen. I've never been in a house this big before."

"It just feels big, but it's really one big circle that always ends up back in the kitchen, which I see you found."

She motioned around the room. "I've never been in a house with a kitchen like this before. I feel like I'm watching Iron Chef or something."

"This kitchen is actually over a decade old. My dad had it redone right before he passed. He was the cook in the family. When he died, I was the only one who ever used it. I'm kind of glad Nick is living here now because the kitchen will get used. I've been thinking about it and if he likes living here, I might offer him the house under market value. Nick has been part of the family since high school. I think it would make my mom and dad happy to know he had the house."

She reached up and rubbed my cheek, the five o'clock shadow brushing her hand. "I think you're an incredibly nice guy, Noel. I'm sure your parents would love that, but where will you live?"

I grasped her hand and held it to my face. "Well, if I get kicked out of that little bungalow with the great view, I'll have to find a new place, but I hope that doesn't happen for a while."

She closed her eyes, her nervousness evident on her face. I couldn't stop myself and I leaned in, letting my lips brush hers. I was careful to avoid the right side but lingered with my lips against hers until she softened and slipped her hand off my face and around my neck. I kept the kiss close-lipped but offered in it what I hoped was a gentle reminder that she deserved kindness and love in a way that didn't hurt. I pulled away slowly and she whimpered, her eyes opening quickly.

"Did I hurt you?" I asked, my hand resting on her cheek.

"No, I just don't think I want you to stop," she whispered.

I smiled and hugged her close to me. "I didn't want to stop. I just want to take it slow, so I don't hurt you."

I felt her nod against my chest, but I didn't let her go. I liked the way she felt in my arms and the way she fits into the middle of my chest when I had my arms wrapped around her. I hoped that keeping her wrapped in my warmth would make her feel safe again.

I rested my chin on her head. "Nick made us a nice dinner, but if you're too tired, I'll understand if you want to crash."

She pulled back a little and I let her go. "No, the nap in the car helped and now I'm hungry. I would hate for that delicious smelling food to go to waste."

"Good, let me get it out and we can eat. Nick kept it warm for us." I busied myself with pulling it from the oven and getting plates down.

"Do you want to eat in the dining room? It seems a little formal." She pointed and I snickered.

The full-size dining table was a little ostentatious, there was no doubt.

I shook my head. "Honestly, I hate that room. It makes me feel all old and stuffy. I thought we could eat on the porch. If you don't mind wearing your coat?"

"There's a porch?" she asked, glancing around the room in surprise.

"There is, but it's off the living room. If you want to grab our coats, I'll take the food out."

She hesitated at the door to the kitchen. I came up behind her and rested my hand on her waist. "Down to the end of the hallway to the front door, coats are in the closet to the left. Go through the door on the left and you're in the living room. You'll see me from there."

"Got it." She laughed and headed down the hall. I watched her walk away, her bottom swaying under the long sweatshirt she wore. I groaned and quickly covered it with a cough when she turned to look at me. I smiled and waved then darted back into the kitchen.

I filled the tray with the food and shut the oven off, leaving the cake in it to stay warm. I met her at the doors to the porch, where she pushed them open for me. I stepped out onto the year-round carpet, stopping at the sight in front of me. Nick had set the table, alright. One of my mother's tablecloths hung flawlessly from the round two-person table with unlit taper candles waiting. There were wine glasses, silverware, and cloth napkins to boot. The wine was in a cooling bucket next to the table. I set the tray down carefully. No wonder I couldn't find the wine, he omitted the part about where the cooler actually was.

"This is gorgeous," Savannah sighed happily.

"I can't take credit for any of this," I admitted. "I asked Nick to throw together some dinner for us. He definitely took it to heart."

I held the chair out for her and she sat, her coat gathered around her shoulders. I noticed the space heater we always used when we were kids and flipped the switch, watching the coil turn red. Soon the porch would be toasty and there would be no need for our coats. I lit the candles with the lighter Nick left and turned the lights off, enjoying the night sky and the lights around the lake.

"What are all those lights out there?" she asked, pointing to the backyard.

I sat in my chair and set her plate in front of her, then half-turned to look out the window. "That's Silver Lake."

She set her fork back down the moment she picked it up. "You live on a lake?"

"No, but my parents' house is on a lake," I reminded her, taking a bite of my chicken. It was so tender it fell apart in my mouth when it hit my tongue. Score one for Nick.

"You really downgraded moving in with me," she mumbled, chewing a piece of carrot.

I lowered my fork and leaned in over the table. "No, I didn't. I traded a beautiful view for a gorgeous one. End of story."

She gave me a little eye roll. "It must have been fun living on a lake as a kid, though."

I shrugged and stabbed more chicken on my fork. "We never really had much time to enjoy it. Someone was always at the café, and once we were old enough, even December and I worked there. I think Mom and Dad planned on this being a retirement place, but that never panned out for them. Deccy and I would bring friends over in the summer when we were in high school, but that was about it."

"A far cry from how I grew up," she said. I wanted to ask but was afraid to ruin the mood. "I think the biggest place I ever lived in had one bedroom. Most were just hotel rooms, and if I was fortunate, we had two beds."

"You moved around a lot?" I asked, pouring some wine in my glass. "Do you want some wine?"

She held her glass out for me to fill. "We moved around a lot, yes. My dad was a user. And by user, I mean of everything; drugs, alcohol, and women. My mom stayed with him, though, heaven forbid she ditch his sorry butt on the side of the road and make a better life for her daughter. I don't think I went to school for more than a month at a time in the same place. Eventually, after a year or two, I would end up back at one of the schools I went to before. Let's just say I never worked too hard at making friends."

I laid my hand over hers on the table. "I'm

sorry. It bothers me to hear about parents who don't put their kids first."

She shrugged a little. "I didn't know anything different, so for a long time, I thought it was normal. It wasn't until I was about thirteen and my dad died from a drug deal gone bad that things started to change. My mom's great aunt worked at McDonald-McMahan High School as a secretary. They had a position open for a janitor and when she heard my father was dead, she somehow got my mom the job. Since my mom was an employee, that meant I got to go to school there without paying tuition."

"Is that a private school?" I asked, not sure what she was talking about.

She laughed sarcastically. "Oh, yes, it's *the* private school in the area. It's where all the *cool rich* kids go."

"Got it." I rolled my eyes a little.

"Yeah, like that. Well, my aunt got us a little one-bedroom apartment and my mom started working. Surprisingly, she enjoyed it and kept on working. I started school in the fall. That's when things really changed because I met Snow."

"Oh, you two went to school together?" I asked, surprised.

"Yes, she was at the school on a scholarship. Her grandmother couldn't afford a school like that, but Snow was beyond gifted and they asked her to come, giving her a free four-year ride. She had the brains to pull it off but felt as awkward as I did about being there. It was harder for her, though. We were both outsiders and didn't have the cool clothes and toys, but she was in a wheelchair to boot. Needless to say, we hit it off the first day. She says it was because I was too skittish to even notice her wheelchair. The truth is, I could tell she was just as scared as I was that everything would fall down around our ears. Of course, she lived with her grandmother and had a great home life. She was smart and beautiful, which was something I wasn't. I was so far behind in school, I barely passed most of my classes the first year, and only because Snow helped me. I used to hang out at Snow's in the evening because my mom worked the three to eleven shift at the school. I could have stayed at my aunt's, but after so many years with no friends, it felt terrific to have one. Do you even care about this?"

"Oh, yes. Please, continue," I encouraged.

"Not much more to say, really. My great aunt passed away my junior year and Snow's grandma did, too. Snow was completely lost after her grandma died."

"Oh, my word. I didn't know about that. All I know is she had polio as a child."

"She contracted polio when her parents were missionaries in the Congo. They came back to the States to get her treatment and stayed in the States for years after that. They did missionary work locally in churches and such, but eventually, they were offered a chance to go abroad again. Their plane crashed in the ocean on the way."

I recoiled and laid my fork down. "That's horrible. I know what it's like to lose a parent suddenly, but then so do you, I guess."

"I didn't lose a parent. I lost dead weight. Maybe that's being disrespectful to my father, but he never acted like a father. He never respected us enough to clean up his life, so I shouldn't have to respect him. I forgave him, but I don't think I have to respect him," she said vehemently.

I was worried she was about to have an attack and went to her, taking her hands in mine and holding her eye. "Tell me about what happened after Snow's grandma died."

Her frown turned to a smile on the left side. "We moved into her grandma's house with her. Mom and I were just living in a little apartment, but my mom was working and saving money. She could afford to do the upkeep on the house since it was paid for. Snow, well, she can't live alone or in just any house. You know."

"Right, she needs help with some things because of her legs," I added and she nodded, giving me a thankful smile.

"Yes. It was the perfect solution because I could help her, and mom could drive us to school. We became like sisters and still are, as you can see by how she loves on me." Her eye had some tears in it and I brushed them away with my thumb.

"I can see the love and mutual respect you have for each other every time you're together. Sunday night, Snow was frantic and I had to calm her down before I could even let her in to see you. She's extremely worried about you." I gave her an upraised brow and she rolled her eye a little.

"She has always been a worrywart. She went off to med school and insisted mom and I stay in the house. I was going to the local business college because hard as Snow tried, you can't fix stupid, and I was stupid."

I shook her hands gently. "Stop. Do not call yourself that ever again. Do you understand me? You are not stupid. Maybe you aren't book smart, but you run a very successful business, and have a beautiful heart."

She was frozen in place, and I was afraid I scared her, but she finally spoke. "I've done some idiotic things in my life, Noel, things that have led me to where I'm sitting today. I deserve this." She motioned at her face. "This is my punishment for being stupid."

My God, did she actually believe that? I shook my head, unsure of how to convince her otherwise. I ran my hand down her cheek, trying to put all the love in my heart into such a simple motion.

"No, Savannah, this is a punishment you don't deserve. This is the result of the actions of a man who doesn't deserve to breathe. I'm sorry if that sounds harsh, but that's how I feel. No man has the right to hit a woman, ever. You didn't deserve this. This didn't happen because you were stupid."

"It did, don't you see? It happened because I

was stupid and married him. Then I was extra stupid and took him back a second time." She tried to pull her hands from mine and I let them go.

"You wanted to be loved, Savannah. There's nothing wrong with that. You wanted to make a go of something you committed to. That's not being stupid, that's being human. We all have things that happen to us that we can look at in two ways. We can look at them as mistakes and never learn anything from them, and be destined to repeat them. Or we can look at them as lessons and learn from them. The question is, was Günther a mistake or a lesson?"

"I always thought he was a mistake, but I did learn a lot about what I want from a relationship, and about myself. So maybe he was a lesson? I learned I want love, but I don't want to sacrifice my safety for love that comes with stipulations or fists. Maybe I'm delusional, but I want a love like Snow and Dully, and December and Jay have. Acceptance of who I am, even if I am a little bit stupid."

"You deserve so much happiness, and maybe the lesson that was Günther will help you recognize real happiness when it comes to you," I suggested softly and she stared into my eyes. Her chin quivered a little bit and I leaned in, cupping it carefully with my hand and laying a kiss on her lips. "You will feel happiness again someday, sweetheart, I promise."

She put her arm around my neck and kissed

me back the best she could. I could taste the sweet wine on her lips and moaned a little when my body reacted to the idea of how delicious the rest of her would taste. I pulled back and rested my forehead on hers. “What happened after Snow went to college?”

I stood up and went back to my seat, shedding my jacket now that the room had warmed up. I had to get away from her before I lost control and let my body take over. I took another bite of chicken to force my mind away from how much I wanted to make love to her.

“She commuted actually, so we lived there together until my mom died in a car accident my last year of business college,” she explained.

“Savannah, I feel horrible for never asking about your parents. I didn’t know you lost both of them.”

She shrugged and played with her fork. “I understand why you didn’t ask about my family life. I don’t have any pictures in my house of them and I don’t offer information freely. That’s because of how I grew up. I loved my mother, but we didn’t have a typical mother-daughter relationship. I was the mother and she was the daughter most of the time. When I lost her, I was sad, but a part of me was relieved. I could finally do whatever I wanted to do. That sounds selfish, but she was like living with a child. I always had to get her up on time, make her lunch, get her to work, and run the household. It was literally like our roles were reversed. I loved her, but she had some major problems. Anyway, don't feel bad about not knowing. I guard my secrets heavily."

"What happened after she died?" I asked, hoping she would talk more about how she got together with Günther.

She laid her fork down on her plate. "My face is sore from talking. Can we just have some dessert?"

I stood up quickly. "Of course, I'll go get it. Molten chocolate lava cake should do the trick."

I picked up her hand and kissed it, then stepped back into the bright light of the living room, wishing the spell hadn't been broken.

Chapter Nine

I locked the front door and turned off the lights on the lower level of the house, double-checking the doors on the porch were locked and then met her at the stairs.

"Let's go upstairs. You can shower first," I promised, picking up our duffel bags. I hadn't been upstairs since we got in, but with three bedrooms available, that left two spare rooms. At the top of the stairs, I stepped in front of her and pushed open the door to Deccy's old room. There was resistance against the door, and when I finally got it open, it was filled with boxes and gym equipment.

She peeked her head in the door. "I don't think Nick has finished unpacking."

I closed the door again and shook my head. "It appears not." I paused a moment and she laughed a little uncomfortably.

"Is there a problem?"

I didn't want to let on that there was a problem, so I shook my head. "Nope, all is well. Let me show you the bathroom and you can shower," I said cheerily, handing her the duffel bag at the door to the guest bathroom. She disappeared inside and I went back to the gym room and pulled out my phone.

I waited while the phone rang and tapped my toe. "Hey, boss!" came Nick's booming voice over the line.

"You're the boss now, remember?" I laughed. "Hey, where's the bed that used to be in the other guest room? It's filled with boxes and gym equipment."

"Oh yeah, it's down in the basement, don't worry, I didn't get rid of it. I figured one guest room was enough and I'm going to make the other room my gym. The guest room is all made up for you. Is there a problem?"

I ran my hand over my face. "No, I was just going to use both rooms tonight."

"Why? You're getting married in a few days. Aren't you sharing a room? Not that it's any of my business," he said, suddenly aware of how it sounded.

I sighed, forgetting for a moment about our little sham. "Her face is bothering her, so I was going to let her sleep alone, but that's okay. No worries."

"Oh, sorry, dude, I didn't think of that. Hey, you can sleep in my bed. I won't be home until after eight. You can use my shower if you want, too," he offered.

I thanked him and hung up the phone. If he wasn't going to be home until eight, I would sleep on the couch and give her the spare bed. I grabbed my duffel bag off the floor and took him up on the shower offer. After dessert, we took a walk down to the lake and the cold January air had chilled me to the bone.

I turned the water on hot and climbed under the spray, the steamy water forcing my eyes closed. I thought about the things she told me tonight. When we were walking, she explained that the house we live in now was Snow's grandmother's house. It was the only home she had ever known, so when Snow wanted to move closer to the hospital, and live more independently, she offered it to Savannah. She wanted to keep the house because it was the only place she ever considered home.

I rubbed the soap around my chest and thought about how this place was always my home, but tonight it didn't feel like it. Tonight, it felt like my parents' home. It was the place I was raised, but not the place I wanted to come home to. Just a short time away told me I need more from life than living in my parent's shadow. While I used to be petrified of that idea, now, I wasn't.

I rinsed the soap off my body, thinking about how I feel when I walk into Savannah's house after being gone for just a few hours. How I throw my coat on the coat rack and grab a beer from the fridge. How I move around the kitchen like I've been there my whole life, cooking meals and watching her read a book on the couch while I clean up. Her house was my home now.

I turned the water off and dried my skin, digging a warm pair of flannel sleep pants from my bag and smoothing a clean long-sleeved shirt over my chest. My long, skinny, and puny chest.

I brushed my teeth and wondered why I cared that my chest was long, skinny, and puny. The kids always called me Gumby when I was a kid, and to be honest, I do resemble him a bit. I thought about Nick and his ripped pecs and six-pack abs I would never have. I guess Savannah's beauty was making my less than picture-perfect body seem more important than I ever thought it was.

I sighed and picked up my bag. *Stop worrying about it, Noel.* I shut off the light and walked through Nick's room to the hallway. She was leaning against the door to the guest bathroom, looking unsure.

"I don't know where you want me to sleep. There's only one bed." She pointed at the guest room.

I took her hand in mine. "Yeah, I thought there would be two rooms. I had no idea he moved one of the beds downstairs. You can have the bed, and I'll sleep on the couch. If you need anything, just call my cell and I'll be right up. Nick won't be home until after eight tomorrow morning."

I steered her toward the guest room, but she stopped about halfway there. "I don't want you to sleep on the couch when you drove here and have to drive again tomorrow. We can, um, can we share the bed?"

"You want to share the bed?"

"I just showered and I won't bite," she promised, holding up her hand in a vow.

I gave her a raised brow. "I'm not worried about you smelling or biting. I'm worried about making you uncomfortable or hurting you."

She took my hand and walked with me to the bedroom. "I trust that you aren't going to hurt me, Noel, and you don't make me uncomfortable. Is it inappropriate to sleep with a man fully clothed when he's about to be your husband? I don't think so."

I turned her around to face me. "You know I'll worry about you the whole night if I sleep downstairs, don't you?"

"Yup, and I don't know why, but I know you will. I would feel better if you actually got some sleep. Tomorrow will be a long day."

I folded the comforter down off the bed and pulled back the sheet, motioning for her to crawl in. She scooted across the bed, and I had to bite my lip as the tank top she was wearing pulled dangerously low over her chest. It covered her, barely, but it left little to my already overactive imagination. She was excellent at hiding it with clothes, but she had a smoking hot body.

I sat down on the bed next to her and set the alarm clock on the bed stand for eight. I wanted enough time to get there, park, and be at the office early.

"Are you going to lie down?" she finally asked. I reached up and turned the lamp off, then pulled the sheet and blankets over us.

I kept my hands to my sides and stayed on my back, afraid to move until she was asleep. If I moved, I might take her in my arms and then where would we be?

"You look like you're dead." She giggled and I turned my head to gaze at her.

"Excuse me?"

She motioned up and down my body. "You're lying there like a mummy. I promise I won't bite," she teased.

I tried to relax and get comfortable, but having her so close to me was not making it easy. Her hand crept across the bed and slipped into mine. "Everything okay?"

"I'm a little scared. I don't like doctors and tomorrow is going to be intense doctors," she whispered. I could hear the fear in her voice and turned onto my side.

"I'll be there with you the whole time. I won't let them hurt you, but we need to find out what's wrong, so we can fix it. I'll keep you safe," I vowed.

"You know when I feel safe?" she asked and I shook my head in the dark, afraid to speak. "I feel safe when your arms are around me. I don't have to worry about anything then."

"It makes me happy to hear you say that. I don't want you to worry about anything. I just want you to get some rest. If you'd like, I'd be happy to put my arms around you," I offered.

"I would like that very much," she whispered and I could hear the tears in her voice.

I sat up and climbed off the bed, pulling her towards me, then climbed over her and settled down behind her.

"What are you doing?" she asked, surprised by the sudden shifting.

I pulled the covers up around us and tucked her in against me, her head on my pillow. "You can't sleep on the right side of your face, so I flipped us around. Now I can hold you all night."

She sighed happily. "You do know how to love me."

I rested my hand over her belly and rubbed it rhythmically with my thumb, not jumping on the words she'd said. I do know how to love her, and if she's starting to recognize it, then that's all I could ask for. I just hoped there was enough distance between us that she couldn't feel what she was doing to me as a man.

She laid her hand over mine. "Good night, Noel."

"Good night, sweet Savannah," I whispered, but she was already asleep.

Savannah

"Hanging in there?" Noel asked after the nurse left the room.

"Thanks to you," I admitted.

He squeezed my hand and kissed my temple.

"Remember, he's here to help you, not hurt you. If you don't understand something, ask him to explain it. I'll be right here."

I nodded my agreement. He was here, and he was with me all night, too. He kept me warm and never let me go, except when he had to get an ice-pack for my face at two o'clock. He's been nothing but patient and loving, and it was easy to get used to. I mean, he's going to marry me to make sure I can get my face repaired. I don't know if it gets more loving and selfless than that. Not that he loves me, loves me, but he does seem to care about me enough to put his life on hold right now.

The door opened and I glanced up from my lap. A man, possibly shorter than I was, entered the room and introduced himself. "Good morning, I'm Dr. Kent."

I shook his hand and then he shook Noel's and sat down on the spinning stool. "Nice to meet you, Dr. Kent. I'm Savannah, and this is my fiancé, Noel Kiss."

"Kiss? Any relation to Kiss's Café?" he asked, his brows going up.

Noel laughed deeply and openly. "One and the same, actually. I just turned the café over to my manager and am opening a new café in Snowberry."

"Oh, you're the white knight." Dr. Kent grinned and I bit back a giggle.

"Excuse me?" Noel stuttered.

"Snow told me a friend would be bringing Savannah today, and you were the white knight of Snowberry. I didn't know what she meant. I get it now. You don't mess with folks' home cooking, and there isn't any in Snowberry proper as it stands. When the café opens, be prepared for a massive onslaught of very hungry townsfolk."

Noel rubbed his hands together. "That's exactly what I'm counting on."

Dr. Kent braced his hands on his thighs. "Snow also told me I had better treat her sister right, or she'd come down here herself."

I dropped my chin to my chest. "I'm so sorry, Dr. Kent. She's so bossy and demanding sometimes."

He started to laugh and shook his head. "Oh, I know. Snow and I go way back as far as medical school. I was scared of her then, and I'm scared of her now, so you can be sure your care here will be the best in the nation."

Noel started to laugh, and soon, we were all giggling. "I feel the same way about Snow," he said. "I love her, but I'm still afraid of her."

I was trying hard not to laugh and aggravate my face, but I was losing the battle quickly. A spasm took hold and wouldn't let go. I moaned, trying to keep my wits about me with the doctor in the room. The pain was searing, as though someone lit my face on fire while pulling as hard as they could upward.

"Breathe, sweetheart," Noel encouraged me. Dr. Kent peeled off the eye patch and the movement made me want to push him away, but Noel had my hands and kept whispering in my ear to let him help. Through the slit in my eye, I could see Dr. Kent's face. It was concerned.

"How long do they last?" he asked me, but Noel had to answer.

"Without ice, she'll be vomiting in a few minutes," he said quickly.

There was a snap and then a cold pack was held to my face. I was so used to the intrusion I didn't even jump. I just prayed the cold would help numb the pain quickly.

"When this spasm ends, she's going to need to rest," I heard Noel tell Dr. Kent. I closed my eyes and fought back nausea that always filled my throat when the attacks happened.

"It's loosening," I was finally able to whisper, and Noel put his arm around me, letting me rest my head on his shoulder.

Dr. Kent rolled in front of me so I could see him. "Snow told me it was severe, but I wasn't expecting this, Savannah. Do you have any double vision?"

"After the bad ones, I do for a few hours out of this eye." I pointed at the right one. "Otherwise, no double vision."

He frowned deeply and sighed. "I don't like this at all. I want you to have an MRI scan immediately." Dr. Kent pushed himself back to the desk where his computer sat.

"Is that necessary?" Noel asked nervously.

"I'm afraid it is. She's presenting with paralysis

of several nerves in her face, and spasms in others. I need to track down exactly what the problem is. Trauma can cause it, but the late-onset is extremely unusual. The MRI will show me if something is compressing the nerves," he explained.

"Like what?" I asked quietly.

"Could be any number of things. The differential includes an aneurysm or blood blister from the trauma, or even a tumor. I won't know until I get the imaging and look at it. Snow told me you don't have insurance, is that correct?" Dr. Kent typed away on the keyboard, not giving us an option about the test.

"Not right now. We're getting married on Saturday and her coverage will be effective immediately," Noel answered quickly.

"That's not a problem. We'll get it all worked out. With the progression Snow described, and after seeing you today, I don't want to wait. Okay?" he addressed me, and I nodded my agreement.

"How will they do the test?" I asked.

He smiled and patted my leg. "They have to put your head in a special brace to hold it in the correct position." I shrunk back against Noel and he took my hand. "Don't look so afraid, you won't remember any of it. You've earned yourself a nice little nap, pretty lady. I will send orders for a sedative and when you wake up, it will be over. Deal?"

I nodded carefully. "Deal. I'm always exhausted after the spasms pass."

He picked up the phone on the wall. "I can see

why. If you've been dealing with that for months now, your system probably has very little to fight them off with." He hung the phone back up without using it. "Follow me and one of our volunteers will get you a wheelchair. I'm going to call down to radiology in a minute and get you in the next available machine. The volunteer will wheel you there and make sure you're in the right place. It's in the other building."

Noel helped me stand up and I leaned against him heavily. I stuck my hand out and Dr. Kent shook it gently. "Thank you, Dr. Kent. I was worried about coming today. I appreciate your candidness and willingness to see me."

"I'm glad, Savannah. Don't lose hope, okay? I know we can figure this out and get you feeling better. Once the MRI is done, you can go get something to eat. I would like to see you again this afternoon. I'll have the nurse call Noel with a time."

I glanced up at Noel. "Can we stay all day?"

"Sweetheart, we can stay for as long as it takes to get you better."

Chapter Ten

Noel

"Let's go for a walk," Savannah suggested when we finally got out of Dr. Kent's office around four.

"Wouldn't you rather go home?" I asked, surprised.

"It has been a really long day and I'd rather we drive back to Snowberry in the morning when it's daylight out if that's okay?" She stopped at the exit of the clinic and zipped up her coat, pulling on her stocking hat and gloves.

I did the same and then kissed her forehead. "If that's what you want, we absolutely can."

She took my hand and we walked out of the building and down the street, going no place in particular. The bustle of the city around the medical center was active, as usual at this time of day. Shuttle buses and taxies ran at dizzying speeds around the medical center. It was warmer than yesterday, and walking was refreshing after spending most of the day in the clinic.

Savannah was given a sedative as promised, and she slept through the MRI with no problems. I used the time to call Snow and give her an update.

She was fretful and scared, so I called December to sit with her. Deccy texted me later that she was okay, Snow just felt useless being so far away.

After Savannah woke up from the MRI, I was able to convince her to eat some lunch, but she mostly picked at it. By the time we got to lunch, the nurse had already called and asked us to be back to his office by two-thirty. I distracted Savannah by touring the rotunda and checking out all the artwork displayed while listening to the pianists play Beethoven and Chubby Checker on the various pianos across the complex.

Dr. Kent didn't have good news when we finally saw him around three. The MRI showed either a tumor or an aneurysm compressing several of her facial nerves. He was hesitant to tell us which but did assure us that if it was a tumor, the characteristics were benign. He felt it could be an aneurysm or build-up of scar tissue from the original injury. Whatever it was, he wanted it out as soon as possible, so we scheduled surgery for a week from today.

"I can't believe he broke my eye socket and I didn't know," she finally whispered. In the din of the city noises, I had to lean in close to hear her. I had her hand and I held it even tighter now. "I remember the pain when he punched me. It was blinding and unlike any pain I'd ever had before. He'd punched me plenty of times, but that time, it just knocked me down. The angle of him being a foot taller than me, and the way he hit me..." she paused and shook her head, swallowing hard. "I sat there on the floor, unable to see anything. Eventually, my vision went back to normal. After a few weeks, I was able to stop covering up the bruises with makeup, but the pain never really went away. Maybe if I had gone in and gotten an x-ray, this wouldn't be happening now."

The anger toward a man I had never met bubbled to the surface, but I had to force it down, so my voice remained calm. "I'm so angry with him I can't even begin to describe it, Savannah. When you can compare the amount of pain you had depending on how hard the blow was, well, it makes me physically ill. It also makes me ill to know you blame yourself for this. I refuse to let you play the what-if game. You did what you had to do to survive."

She stopped walking and glanced up at me. "Isn't that what we're doing? Playing the what-if game? We're getting married because of it."

I pulled her into me, our coats keeping me from feeling the warmth of her body I had come to long for. "I'm marrying you in a few days so you can have surgery next week. We have our answers now, and we need to move forward knowing we made the absolute right decision."

I leaned down and kissed her lips gently. They were cold from the chilled air but warmed quickly as soon as mine lingered and warmed them. She sighed a little from somewhere deep inside and snuggled closer to me. I pulled my lips off hers but kept my head low. “Speaking of getting married, we were supposed to get our rings today. Would you rather wait and go tomorrow?”

“We should go get them tonight. Maybe it would take our minds off things?”

“Sounds good to me, and I know just the place.” I grinned, turning her around. The door in front of us said, Lasker Jewelers.

“Well, that’s convenient.” She giggled and I retook her hand, swinging it as we walked to the door.

“I thought so.”

“Remember, just a simple band. Nothing expensive,” she fretted and I held her hands in front of her and kissed her nose.

“How about whatever you like, and whatever it costs, is fine,” I joked and pulled the door open, ushering her inside.

A man glanced up from behind one of the counters. “Welcome to Lasker. Can I help you find something today?”

I moved in closer and his face registered recognition. “Noel, how the heck are you?”

He came around the edge of the counter and gave me a quick man-hug, slapping my back.

“I’m good, Toby. Busy as ever, but good.” I smiled at Savannah and she stared down at the floor, letting her hair fall over her cheek.

“I talked to Nick the other night and he said you were off opening a new café. Where are you at this time?” Toby inquired.

"Snowberry, actually. Have you heard of it?"

"Snowberry?" A voice from behind us piped up. "That's a great little town. I was there for their Winter Fest this past Christmas and the sweetest thing happened. A guy proposed to his girlfriend on stage."

I turned to see an older lady polishing the glass of a display case. I walked over and stuck my hand out. "I'm Noel Kiss, and that girl was my twin sister, December."

The woman shook my hand and stopped mid-shake when I finished my sentence. "No way! What a coincidence. He was so romantic getting down on his knees like that," she gushed.

I smiled at Savannah and tucked my arm around her waist. "Jay definitely got his girl with that little move. They married on Christmas Eve, and we just celebrated with them at their reception last weekend."

"I bet it was so romantic. There's this little flower shop in the town and she always has the best flowers. I bet the whole wedding was filled with flowers."

"It was beautiful, and I would guess you're referring to Savannah's Flower Emporium? The flower shop, I mean."

She snapped her fingers. "That's the name, yes. Such a quaint, unique little shop."

I motioned to Savannah with my free hand. "Meet Savannah, owner and operator of Savannah's Flower Emporium."

Savannah was trying to make herself as tiny as possible, but I would have nothing of it. Her business was something to be proud of and I wouldn't let her downplay its success.

The woman held her hands to her mouth. "No way!" She finally stuck her hand out in Savannah's direction and Savannah shook it, trying to smile.

"Nice to meet you. I'm Savannah Hart, I didn't catch your name." Savannah waited and the woman finally snapped out of her surprise.

"Yes, sorry, my name is Kay, and you already know Toby. What can we do for you two tonight? Looking for anything in particular?"

I spoke up before Savannah could. "Actually, we're looking for wedding bands. We're getting married on Saturday."

In my peripheral vision, I could see Toby pulling out trays from under the counter.

Kay clapped excitedly. "Congratulations! Well, let's see what we have for you. Toby will help you fit yours, and I'll help Savannah."

She scooted from behind her display case and stood next to Toby. We followed her over and stared at the mind-boggling choices for wedding bands.

"What kind of solitaire are you wearing, dear?" Kay asked Savannah.

"I, uh, I don't have a solitaire. I just want a band," she stuttered, and the woman looked at her a bit funny.

"No engagement ring?" she asked, but the

question was directed at me. Now it was my turn to sweat a little.

"I wanted Savannah to come with me and pick out the ring she wants. She does a lot of work with her hands in the flower shop, so I didn't want to get something that wouldn't work," I rambled.

Savannah had wandered off to another display case and was staring intently at something under the glass.

"I see," Kay said, but her tone of voice said she didn't approve. "Usually the man picks the solitaire and then you pick the bands as a couple."

"Well, we aren't your usual couple," I said pointedly, and Toby moved in instantly.

"No two couples are alike, Noel. I completely understand what you're saying and it makes sense to me. I see a lot of couples who come in looking for the perfect ring because one or the other has an occupation that requires just the right ring. Let me show you some of the choices and maybe you'll find what's right for you," he offered, pushing one of the small black pads forward.

"Savannah, should we get matching ones?" I asked her, but her head was bent down even closer to the glass now. I held my finger up to Toby and went over to the case. "Savannah?"

I glanced down at what she was staring so intently at. It was a beautiful band with vines and diamond-encrusted roses. There was a pinkish hue to it, making the flowers look almost real. I laid my hand on her back and she finally glanced up at me.

"Oh, sorry, I got distracted." She grimaced, motioning me back toward the other counter, but I held my ground.

"Can we see this ring?" I pointed at it and Kay came over to where we were standing.

"That's actually an anniversary band," she pointed out, and I looked at her cross-eyed.

"Is there a law that says you can't use an anniversary band for a wedding band?" I asked, tired of her inability to think outside the box.

Savannah put her hand on my arm. "No, it's okay, Noel. She's right, let's look over there." She tried to push me that direction, but I refused to budge.

Kay must have gotten the hint because she quickly unlocked the case and took out the band, setting it on the counter. Toby moseyed over and pulled the band off the display pad.

"This is one of my favorite pieces. It's the rose scroll ring. This one is made of rose gold. We have it in silver and regular gold as well. There's nearly a half-carat diamond in the ring itself. It's really quite stunning." He handed it to me and I nodded, taking Savannah's left hand and slipping it on her ring finger.

"Look, a perfect fit."

She stared down at the ring, bringing it closer to her eye to see. "I've never seen anything this beautiful, and I see beautiful things all day, every day," she whispered, her eyes intent on the large rose in the middle.

"I've never seen anything as beautiful as you are wearing it. I think it should come home with us." I smiled and she glanced up quickly then, the spell broken.

She shook her head and took the ring off, handing it back to Toby. "Excuse us for a minute."

Toby and Kay nodded, a knowing smile on their face as Savannah pulled me over toward the other counter. "You can't buy that ring. Did you see how much it costs?" she whisper-exclaimed.

"I don't care how much it costs. The ring is beautiful, you love it, it describes who you are all in one ring, and it fits you like a glove. You deserve it, and if you want it, it's yours," I said firmly.

"What do you mean it describes me?"

"Tell me what the symbolism is behind a rose. I know you know this." I smiled, kissing her hand.

She stared at me funny but finally relented and answered. "Roses supposedly represent love, honor, beauty, devotion, wisdom, faith, timelessness, and some say passion and sensuality," she recited, her eye in a squint while she tried to figure out my point.

"That pretty much describes you, in my opinion. You love so many people in the little town of Snowberry, you honor them every time you send flowers to special events and funerals without being asked." Her face held a look of surprise and I kissed her nose. "Yes, I know about that. You're beautiful beyond words, devoted to the people you love, have more faith right now than a lot of people have in a lifetime, and you definitely have an underlying sense of passion and sensuality that my body reacts to every time I kiss you."

"You do?" she asked, shocked.

"Haven't you noticed every time I kiss you that it's all I can do to hold myself back from kissing every part of you? I've taken more cold showers in the last month than I've ever taken in my life, but I still can't stay away from you. I have to touch you, feel your warmth, so I know I'm alive."

To prove my point, I leaned down and kissed her lips passionately. It was a short kiss, one that said *I want you* in a matter of seconds, but one that wasn't going to embarrass us in front of others. I drew away from the kiss and hugged her close, pressing my hips into hers. I laid my mouth near her ear. "Do you feel what you do to me with just one kiss?"

She nodded, clearing her throat, but she kept hold of me. Her arms loosely wrapped around me, making it look like I was whispering to her about the ring.

"I would love nothing more than to act on my desires on our wedding night, but I won't because I know that's not why we're getting married. That said, if you walk away from this experience with one lesson, let it be this; never underestimate your beauty and self-worth. You're beautiful, and you deserve the best life has to offer you. Don't shy away from it because you think you're not good enough. You're better than good enough, you're perfect." I pulled back and looked her in the eye. It was filled with tears and her chin trembled. I wiped away the tears with my thumb and kept my eyes on her until she stiffened her spine and nodded once.

She had my shirt fisted in her hand and gazed up at me, her face filled with honesty and innocence. "I love the ring. Do you think we can find something to compliment it for you?"

I grabbed her and hugged her tightly, swaying her back and forth while laughing. "Yes, I think we can!"

I gave Toby a thumbs up behind her back, and he did a fist pump in the air, pulling the ring from the display and handing it to Kay. When she walked away, even she couldn't hide her smile.

Savannah

"Thanks for coming with me today, ladies. I'm not good at picking out clothes for myself," I admitted and Snow groaned then covered it with a cough.

"You don't say?" she asked, looking me up and down. I glanced down at my outfit.

"What? Do I not match? Is something wrong with what I'm wearing?" I asked frantically.

December laughed from the back seat. "There's nothing wrong with what you're wearing, Savannah. Snow is just messing with you."

"She's right, I'm just messing with you, but mostly because I'm trying not to yell." Snow grinned and I gave her a look.

"Yell about what?"

"You just thanked us for coming along with you to find your wedding dress. As if you were going to go shop for a dress alone. That just wouldn't do."

I snickered and held my hands up. "Sorry, this is a bit of a rush job, but I would never go dress shopping without you. Ever," I promised, crossing my heart.

"From what I hear, if we did let you go alone, you'd buy a denim smock that you could wear again at the shop," December said from the back, and I turned in my seat.

"Oh, is that right? Who, pray tell, told you that?" I asked snootily.

"My brother, you know that guy you're marrying. He says you don't own anything quote, *frilly*." She grinned, flinging her hands around while making air quotes.

I wanted to argue, but I really couldn't because I don't own anything frilly. "He's right. I don't do frilly. I hope he's not looking for frilly because it's so not happening."

Snow started to giggle, and pretty soon, she was laughing so hard she was wiping away the tears as she pulled into the parking lot of Ann's. "Okay, no frilly, just promise me you'll be open-minded about this. We only have today and tomorrow to find a dress."

I sighed. "I really could just wear something I already have."

Snow leveled a look at me. "You're getting married. You can't wear jeans and a sweatshirt. Let's go," she ordered, pointing out the door. I saluted her jauntily and climbed out while December helped her get out on the ramp.

In a matter of minutes, I found myself standing in the middle of the land of frilly.

"Good heavens," I groaned, heading for the door, but Snow blocked my way with MAC.

"We can find something not frilly, but you have to look," she insisted.

December hooked her arm in mine, so I couldn't run. "There are some evening gown type dresses in the back. Is that what you're looking for?"

I nodded my head. "Yes, I just want a simple dress. It's a Saturday afternoon, and I don't need anything super expensive and fancy. Maybe even something I can wear again."

Snow motored MAC through the aisles and waved at Ann, who was helping another bride. She assured us she would be right there, but to start looking. If shopping for a ring wasn't real enough, shopping for a dress was driving it home that this was happening. I was marrying Noel the day after tomorrow and I didn't have a choice. If I didn't marry him, I was going to go bankrupt and lose the emporium. I also knew that marrying him meant he had to take care of me and pay for something my first husband did to me. It was a no-win situation.

"God, this is so unfair," I whispered, the dresses blurring in my vision.

"What, honey?" December asked sweetly.

I glanced at her, realizing I had said it aloud. "All of this. It's so unfair to Noel. Look at me," I whispered, covering my good side. "Look at this. Why is he doing this?"

December pulled me into a hug and moved me toward a dressing room, sitting me on the small bench. Snow rolled in and closed the door behind us.

"My brother is marrying you because he loves you," December reminded me, and I laughed weakly, shaking my head. I knew the truth. He was marrying me out of pity. I had to be honest with myself and admit I wanted him to love me, but I knew the truth.

"What if, though?" I asked and December cocked her head.

"What if what?" she asked.

"What if the surgery doesn't fix my face and he's stuck with me like this forever?" I breathed out, the question sticking in my throat.

"He loves you, Savannah, and when you love someone, you don't see their imperfections. Sometimes those imperfections are the reason you love the person. You know they're stronger than you could ever be and you want to offer them whatever comfort you can. I feel that way with Jay and I bet Dully feels the same way about Snow."

Snow laid her hand on my leg. "She's right, you know. And every woman is nervous before her wedding. Let's face it, you haven't known Noel very long. I understand why you're scared, but Noel is marrying you in sickness, so imagine what it will be like in health."

I registered her words but didn't respond. I knew when I was healthy, he would be free, and that scared me. Once I was healthy, he wouldn't be my husband anymore and I'd have to see him every day. That would kill me slowly. *Keep it together, Savannah. Find a dress and then you can go home.*

I straightened my spine and stood. "You're right. I'm just nervous and the medication is making my mind fuzzy and tired. Let's go before Ann gets worried." I tried to smile, knowing full well it wouldn't work, but it seemed to comfort Snow. She turned and rolled out of the room with December and me trailing behind her.

There were so many dresses that I didn't quite know where to start. Noel insisted I take two hundred dollars from him to pay for the dress, and even though I refused, I know December had it in her pocket.

"Did you stop by the house and pick up the things Noel brought from Rochester?" I asked December as we looked through racks of evening gowns.

"I stopped and picked it up the other day. I didn't know he still had all of that stuff. Did he show you any of it?" she asked, her hand on a gown.

"He showed me the baby outfits. I can't believe he was ever that small," I snickered.

"He was smaller than me when he was born!" She laughed and shook her head. "That changed quickly. By the time we were one, he was head and shoulders above me. I was no longer the big sister."

"I'm glad he saved it for you. He really feels terrible about how poorly he treated you," I told her, hoping it would make her feel better to know he really did regret it.

She took me by the shoulders and looked me in the eye. "Grief changes people. It makes them close up inside, afraid to love on the off chance they get hurt again. I understood that was how Noel was dealing with my mother's death. I hoped someday he would come around. Eventually, grief turns to acceptance and when that happens, you can move on."

She dropped her hands and I patted her face. "Point taken, my dear. I'm just happy for you both. Noel is going to make a great uncle to all the little ones to come."

"Are you kidding me? He's going to be a bigger pushover than Uncle Jay." She snickered so Snow couldn't hear us. "Did he tell you he has more stuff at the Rochester house and invited me out there in the spring to go through it?"

I shook my head but smiled. “No, he didn’t, but I’m glad. It makes me happy that you can put everything behind you in order to share the future.”

My voice trailed off when I finally found Snow in front of a rack, holding a dress out, frozen in place.

December grasped my arms and sighed. “I have goosebumps,” she whispered.

Snow hung it on the rack to display it and clapped her hands a little. “The first dress we find and it’s nothing short of perfect. You have to try this on.”

“Isn’t that gorgeous?” Ann asked, coming around the corner. “I got some of those in about a week ago. I thought they would be perfect for the formal coming up at the high school.”

“Savannah wants to try this one on,” Snow spoke for me and I gave Ann the palms up.

“I guess I want to try it on. What sizes do you have?” I asked.

“That’s the only one I have. I don’t even know what size it is,” she admitted, taking it off the rack and checking the tag. “Size eight.”

Snow motioned towards the dressing room. “That’s her size! I’m telling you, Savannah, it’s meant to be.”

I rolled my eye a little and followed the parade to the dressing room, where Ann looped the dress over the hook and removed the plastic sack. “I’ll let your ladies in waiting help, but if you need anything just give me a shout."

Snow agreed and closed the door behind her as I stared at the dress. It was cream, tea length, and had little cap sleeves over the shoulders.

"I bet this would look amazing with that crocheted wrap you have," Snow gushed as December took it down off the hanger.

I stripped down to my underwear and slipped into the dress, zipping the zipper on the side. Standing in front of the mirror, I stared at the pink roses that cascaded down the green vines, wrapping around the dress in a spiral. Snow was right, the dress was perfect.

I smoothed my hands over the chest and down to the waist, stepping closer to the three-way mirror, turning so I could see the back. It fit like a glove and it was made for me.

"It's like the ring," I finally realized, turning to see the way the pattern spiraled around the dress.

"What ring?" December asked and I turned.

"Noel took me shopping to pick out my ring when we were in Rochester yesterday. I noticed a ring and he caught me staring at it. It was ridiculously expensive, but it fit perfectly, so he insisted we get it. The band is wrapped with diamond roses."

Snow wheeled behind me and wrapped her arms around my waist. "I can't wait to see it on your finger. I also can't wait to see Noel's face when he catches a load of you in this dress."

December leaned against the wall facing us. "It

fits perfectly, just like the ring, which means it's meant to be."

I glanced back to the mirror. "Maybe he won't notice my face as much if I wear this dress."

Snow hugged me tighter. "Nice try, have you seen the way he looks at you? All he sees is the woman he loves. This dress is going to wow him, but it's the woman wearing it that makes it beautiful."

December grinned. "I'm with Snow."

"Is it legal to buy the first dress you try on?" I joked and they both laughed.

"When it's this gorgeous, yes." Snow laughed, finally releasing me.

I grimaced a little. "I didn't even check the price." I searched around the dress for a tag, feeling around the back of the neck, but there wasn't one.

Snow snickered and then gave December a high five. "Ann already has the price tag and my credit card." Her phone dinged and she looked at the readout. "And like that, the dress is yours."

"Snow, no. No, you can't buy this dress!" I exclaimed.

"I just did, so that means I can. Please, let me do this for you, Savannah. I love you so much and I know you're already stressed out about everything that's happening. I want you to look and feel as beautiful as you are in here," she said, patting her chest. "Consider it a gift from your sister for your wedding day."

I had no words for the woman who sat in

front of me. The same woman who had gotten me through so many rough times in my life. I knelt next to her chair and hugged her tightly. “I love you so much, Snow.”

“I love you too, Savan. Happiness is yours again with Noel. You’ve suffered enough, and I know you have more to go through, but Noel will love you through sickness and health.”

I didn’t speak, just kept my face hidden in her neck because for just a few moments, I wanted to believe the promise in her words.

Chapter Eleven

Noel

I knocked on her bedroom door and waited. When I heard a soft *come in,* I pushed the door open and carried the tray through the door.

She sat up in bed and pulled the Velcro apart on the special icepack Dr. Kent had given us last week. Thankfully, it helped her sleep through the night without pain waking her up. She got more rest, and that helped keep the attacks at bay.

"Good morning, my future wife." I smiled, setting the tray down on the dresser near her bed.

"Good morning, my future husband," she replied sleepily. "I think it's against tradition to see each other before the ceremony."

I sat down on the edge of the bed and tucked a piece of hair behind her ear. She didn't have the eye patch on and she tried to cover her face, but I pulled her hand down. "Don't do that. Give me a chance to see you, really see you. You're stunning in the morning." Her good eye closed and she nodded, but I knew she didn't believe me. "As for tradition, it may be against it, but I don't think we're doing very much of this traditionally. Besides, in a lot of cultures, the bride and the groom walk to the ceremony together, enjoying some special quiet time alone before they get married. I'm all about that, so I brought you breakfast."

I stood and got the tray, setting it over her lap and tucking a couple pillows behind her back.

"You spoil me." She smiled, taking a sip of the tea and eyeing the toast and eggs. "Aren't you going to eat?"

I shook my head. "My stomach is a little nervous, but I had some tea and toast. You need to take your medication, so please eat a little."

"Your stomach is nervous?" she asked, swallowing the new medication Dr. Kent had given her with some juice. "Why are you nervous?"

"I've never gotten married before. I don't want to screw up."

She put her hand over her heart and feigned shock. "You've never been married before? I had no idea." She winked and I chuckled.

I rubbed her leg under the blanket and encouraged her to eat. "I thought about it once, but it didn't work out."

She set the toast down and wiped her hands. "Oh? Who was she?"

I leaned back on my palms. "Her name is Alana. We dated through the last few years of high school and then off and on for the next few years when I opened a café in the town she moved to. We gave it a real go, but after about six months, I realized I didn't love her enough to give up the café and house in Rochester. If it came down to it, I would give her up for those things, which meant she wasn't the right woman for me."

She sighed. "Wish I had done that. It takes a lot of maturity to be honest with yourself about relationships that aren't meant to be. I never should have married Günther. I knew it then as much as I know it now, but I thought I could change him. Typical abused woman thinking, from what I hear. The old saying *you live what you learn* couldn't be more accurate. I watched my mother do it and I turned around and did the same thing."

I took her hand and kissed it softly. "You have to let the past go and know in here," I tapped her chest, "he wasn't the one for you."

"You can say that again," she mumbled, taking a bite of eggs.

"He wasn't the one for you." I winked and she shook her head at me while she chewed.

"Has there been anyone since Alana?"

"Not seriously, no. I dated a few women now and again, but very few understand the time commitment involved in operating a café. If I had to cancel a date, or something came up while we were out, they rarely understood. You know what I mean?"

"Yeah, I get it. Not that I've dated since my divorce, but I imagine it would be the same for me. I work long hours and when I'm not at the emporium, I'm usually doing something for it. The workload has improved over the last year, though.

I have the business running smoothly, so I get a lot more done during the day."

I traced a finger down the good side of her face and dropped it to her shoulder. "You haven't dated since the divorce? I'm surprised to hear that. There had to be plenty of men who wanted to take you out."

She laughed a little self-consciously. "Oh, there were some offers, but I wasn't ready. I was embarrassed that everyone knew I let my husband beat me."

"No." I shook my head. "No, you didn't give him permission to hit you. That's all on him. You will not carry the blame for his inability to be a man. Do you understand me?"

"I try, Noel, I really do, but it affects how I deal with men. I'm afraid to be alone with them, especially in my house when no one is around. It's just easier to decline the offers with a smile."

I motioned around the room. "We're alone in your house, and I'm a man. Do I make you afraid?" She shook her head no. "Why not?"

She shrugged her shoulder. "You just don't. You treat me like you care about me, not just like you want to get me into bed."

I struggled with keeping my expression neutral. "I do care about you, Savannah, a lot. I want you to get better and I'll do whatever I have to in order to make that happen."

She set the tray next to her on the bed and sat up. "Like marry the monster that is me today."

I pulled her to me and laid my lips on her lazy eye. She recoiled and tried to push me away, but I wouldn't let her. I wasn't hurting her, so I feathered kisses down her eye and to the lips that couldn't move. I used my own lips and made love to them until she relented and opened her mouth, letting me taste the sweet tea on her tongue. She moaned softly and I pulled her onto my lap, angling her head so I could continue to kiss her lips without hurting her. When I pulled back, I was breathing heavily and she surely could feel the bulge in my pants. "You're not a monster. Promise me you won't ever call yourself that again." She laid her head on my chest and nodded against it. "I'm marrying you because I want to, no other reason. Do you understand?"

"I do understand, Noel, maybe more than you'll ever know," she whispered.

I set her back on the bed and pulled a box out of my pocket. "I got you something for our wedding. It's your something new."

She reached for it and then pulled her hand back. "You weren't supposed to get me anything. I didn't get you anything."

I encouraged her to take the box. "I didn't expect you to get me anything. There's nothing I need. I just wanted you to know I'm always thinking about you."

She finally took the box, and I noticed her hand shake a little when she pulled the paper off. The Lasker emblem was on the front and she glanced up at me. "What else did you buy?"

"Open it and you'll find out."

She smiled and finally pulled the box open to reveal the necklace inside. Her hand started to shake as she reached for the chain, but then brought her hand to her mouth instead. "It's an angel."

"Yes, it is," I answered. "When I saw it, I just knew you had to have it."

"Because you call me your angel," she whispered, a tear falling down her face.

I swiped it away and nodded. "You are my angel. Whenever you get scared, you can look at it and remember that you matter to me. You are my angel."

"You don't know how much this means, Noel. No one has ever done anything this nice for me. Like no one, ever."

I took the box from her hand and pulled the chain off the pad carefully. "I'm glad I got to be the first. May I?" I asked, holding it out.

She nodded and I fastened it around her neck and let my hands drop to her shoulders. She closed her eye and put her hand over the angel.

"Do you feel it?" I asked.

She didn't need to answer, I could see it in the way her shoulders relaxed and her breathing evened out.

"Noel, you may kiss your bride," the minister said with great enthusiasm.

I grinned, finally getting to take this beautiful woman into my arms.

"Thank God," I whispered, then kissed her carefully, surprised when she wrapped her arms around my neck and kissed me with all she had.

The audience clapped and whistled loudly until we pulled apart and turned to the much larger crowd than we had expected to attend.

"Ladies and gentlemen, I give you Mr. Noel and Savannah Kiss."

Snow handed Savannah her bouquet, and I took her arm, walking down the stairs of the band shelter and through the throng of people who were throwing confetti as we ran to the waiting car. We climbed in the back and our chauffeur chirped the tires as he pulled away.

"Oh, my gosh!" Savannah exhaled. "Where did all those people come from?"

Our yet unnamed chauffeur chuckled without turning. "When word got out that the lady who spreads the most cheer in our town was getting married, well, we had to celebrate with you. Hope you don't mind that we changed the venue without your permission."

"Tom, is that you?" Savannah leaned forward, trying to get a look at him.

"You know it, girl. I'm taking you to a secret location where you will have pictures taken with your husband, and then rejoin your wedding reception for a home-cooked meal, thanks to Kiss's Café." He turned the car and pulled up in front of the walkway to the lake.

"Pictures?" Savannah whispered, her eye as big as a saucer.

"Thanks, Tom. We won't be long," I assured him, helping her out of the car. He pulled away and parked, dousing the lights.

"Pictures? We didn't plan pictures," she whispered frantically.

I held her shoulders and kissed her softly. "I know we didn't plan pictures, but we want this to look real, right? I know the wedding was rushed, but everyone has someone take pictures on their wedding day," I reminded her and she hung her head down, staring at my shoes. "Sweetheart, this dress is so amazing I simply can't let you get away without some pictures. When I saw you walking toward me, you took my breath away."

Her hand went back to her neck where her necklace was, and she smiled in the darkness. "Okay, just a few pictures. Wait, did he say reception?"

I took her hand and held it loosely. "Yes, he said reception. It's just a small gathering at the hall. Everyone was so excited about being part of our day that I couldn't say no. They love you here, Savannah, don't you see that?"

She glanced around a little and shivered. "I do, but I feel like I'm deceiving them. Everyone is so supportive, and we're..."

My lips came down on hers before she could finish the sentence. If she didn't say it, then I could continue to pretend I just married the woman of my dreams and she would be mine forever, instead of just for a little while. Her hands held my tie, pulling me closer, and my arms found their way around her waist. It took me more than a few seconds to recognize the sound of clicking. I glanced up, tucking Savannah against me to hide her face.

"Don't stop on my account." The visitor laughed, and I breathed a sigh of relief.

"Bram, you scared the daylights out of me," I exclaimed, relief coursing through me. I extended my hand to him and he shook it firmly. "Thanks for offering to take the pictures."

"I'm happy to do it. After all, it's what I do for a living. I'll even make sure the best shot gets in the paper for your announcement." He smiled and Savannah glanced up embarrassedly.

She waved at Bram. "Hi, sorry about the PDA. Newly married and all that."

Bram was sucking in his cheeks to keep from laughing. "No need to apologize, Savannah. I got some great shots and you weren't even trying. Those are the shots that always turn out the best."

He motioned for us to follow him down the path to the small bridge that crossed a stream parallel to the lake. It struck me that though it was frozen on both sides, there was a small trickle in the middle that kept flowing.

"The bridge has natural light from the moon. I've been waiting for a couple with a night wedding to get some of these pictures." He clapped excitedly, placing us just so on the bridge. He didn't wait for a response just started taking pictures. I noticed on every shot that Savannah was turned in toward me, so you only saw the left side of her face.

"One last picture, guys. Noel, lift her up to sit on the railing and hold her waist. Savannah, look deeply into his eyes, away from the camera. There's a moonbeam about to hit us." He was giddy with excitement, so not to disappoint him, I backed her up to the railing and hoisted her up to the top rail. She braced her feet on the lower rail and rested her arms around my neck.

She leaned her forehead against mine but didn't say a word. I raised one hand and brushed a tear from her eye just as the moonbeam swept across her face.

"Right now, at this moment, I wish I could always be your bridge," I sighed.

I gazed into her eyes when her lips came down on mine, and they told me she wished the same.

The house was quiet when we got home and I enjoyed the sound of silence for the first time all day. The reception was an unexpected way to meet a lot of people in town all at once. April was great at pointing out Buck's previous employees, so I could be sure to touch base with them. I'm not one to mix business with pleasure, but in this case, it was necessary. I have an immediate need to line up good help, and with her surgery coming in a few days, I didn't have much time.

By the time the evening was over, I had a head cook, three waitresses, and a prep cook. The smartest thing I ever did was hire April to be my manager. She grew up here and knew everyone. She mingled among them, and before I knew it, people were seeking me out. I had no doubt I'd made the best decision of my life coming here.

The clock on the microwave read eleven when I made her tea. I sent her straight to the shower when we got home, worried if she didn't relax soon, her face was going to revolt. I grabbed her pills and ice pack on the way to her room and stopped in the doorway. My wife was doubled over on the bed, wrapped in a towel, her body shaking. It took three steps to reach her and I grabbed for her, her body still slick from the shower. In one motion, she was on the bed and the icepack was on her face.

"You're doing okay," I whispered calmly, "Ice is on now, just relax and breathe slowly. In and out, in and out." I talked her through the pain until it began to subside, and she sagged against me. "I knew tonight was going to be too much. You need your medication and some rest."

She also needed clothes because the sight of her body when the towel fell away was causing me pain. I grabbed her robe off the end of the bed and helped her shrug it on.

"Usually, the husband is taking the robe off on the wedding night," she sighed glibly.

"Call me an unusual husband then, but you're in pain." I ground out, trying to keep my need from overtaking my common sense.

I laid her back on the pillows and rubbed her leg while the ice did its job. Once she was comfortable again, I helped her take the pills.

"I only had one attack today," she pointed out.

"I was worried all day, but you did great. I'm proud of you for not letting it stop you from enjoying the day. You did enjoy the day a little, right?" I asked, more for myself than for her.

"I enjoyed the day a lot," she admitted, her right hand twirling the ring on her left hand. I picked up her left hand and kissed her ring finger, the metal cold against my lips.

"Good, because I did, too. I know we aren't a traditional couple, but when I pledged to love you in sickness and in health, it meant something special to me." My eyes drifted to the band on my own hand and I remembered the words I promised today. I knew at some point I would break them, but for tonight I would continue to honor them.

"I want to thank you for everything you've done to help me, Noel," she whispered, then took the icepack off and scooted over, loosening my tie.

Her eyes never strayed from mine until it was untied and on the bed. She opened the top button of my shirt and I grasped her hand gently.

"What are you doing?" I asked breathlessly.

"Thanking you," she answered before going up on her knees and kissing me hard. She pushed me back on the bed and lay half on top of me, her robe open in the front and her breasts pressing against the thin material of my shirt, leaving burning streaks of heat across my chest.

My mind went blank and my hands wound their way into her hair, holding her lips to mine and drinking every last drop of nectar she had to offer. She moaned against my lips and ground her hips into mine. That's when the clanging bells rang in my ears, and I ripped my mouth from hers.

I held her chin carefully. "We can't do this, sweetheart." I gazed into her eyes, but hers darted away from mine.

She crawled off me and moved back to the bed, wrapping her robe around herself and slipping under the covers. "Of course, I'm sorry. I don't know what came over me thinking you wanted to make love to this."

"Stop, right now," I bellowed, and she jumped back against the bed. I took a deep breath and held my hands out to her. "I'm sorry, I didn't mean to scare you, but I can't stand it when you degrade yourself." I scooted closer to her and took her hand, laying it against the bulge in my pants. "Does this feel like I don't want you?"

She ran her hand instinctively over me and I closed my eyes, swallowing hard. Her soft *no,* finally brought me back to reality.

"That's because I want you more than I've ever wanted a woman before in my life."

"Then what's stopping you?" she asked desperately.

"The idea that if and when we consummate this marriage, it will be because of love, not lust, fear or gratitude."

She glanced down at the ring on her finger and away from my eyes. "You think I'm afraid."

I scooted close to her and took her in my arms. "I know you're afraid, and there's nothing wrong with needing the touch of a person who cares about you when you're afraid. I will stay with you all night long and keep you safe in my arms, Savannah. You don't have to give yourself to me in order to feel safe."

"That's not fair to you," she whispered, her eyes misty.

I kissed her lips gently, lovingly, and chastely. "Savannah, I long for the nights I get to hold you in my arms. Tuesday night, I didn't sleep a wink because I spent the whole night memorizing every little thing about you. I don't need the act of sex to be intimate with you. Having you in my arms is enough for me right now, okay?"

She nodded and I pulled back slowly. "I'm going to go take a shower, a cold shower actually," I joked and she finally smiled. "Then, if you don't mind, I'm going to sleep in here tonight with you in my arms."

Chapter Twelve

"More coffee, Mr. Kiss?" I glanced up into the face of the kind elderly volunteer who was in the surgical waiting room. I stared down at my cup and saw that it was empty, but I had no memory of drinking it.

"Sure, thank you." I held the cup out and she filled it.

"I know it seems like this is taking a long time, but Dr. Kent is an excellent surgeon and he always takes his time. Don't be worried," she encouraged, patting my shoulder and moving on.

The room had emptied out since I first got there, and I was the only one left from the first round of surgery patients this morning. New people streamed in and out of the room, but silence prevailed and it was starting to get on my nerves. I needed to hear something soon, or I might lose my mind.

I was exhausted and also hyped up on coffee. I know Savannah didn't sleep last night because I was awake holding her. This morning, when I brought her to the clinic for surgery, she put on a brave face, but she was clearly in distress. When they finally got her I.V. started, and gave her something for the anxiety, she relaxed and drifted in and out of sleep until Dr. Kent came in to see us. I heard the words he told us but saw the truth in his eyes. This was serious, and the ramifications could be something she deals with for the rest of her life.

I stretched my feet out in front of me and rested my hands behind my head, glancing at my phone on the chair next to me. Snow, December, and half of Snowberry had already texted or called looking for an update. No one wanted one more than me at this moment, though.

April instilled herself behind Savannah's counter Sunday morning and insisted we take the few days before surgery to run away for a honeymoon. It was slightly awkward explaining that to Savannah, but surprisingly, she packed her bags and requested we go to my house in Rochester.

We spent the last few days sleeping, walking by the lake holding hands, and getting to know each other better. We ate at the café every night, and Nick made us breakfast the last few mornings. We snuggled under a blanket on the couch watching movies, and looked through the old photo albums left inside the coffee table. We did what newly married people do, except for the one thing I really wanted to do. She wasn't in the right place for it, and I wasn't about to take advantage of her when she was vulnerable.

I closed my eyes and saw her face right before they came and took her in for surgery. It was soft and relaxed for the first time in three days. She had half a smile on her face and she wouldn't let go of my hand. I walked with her as far as they would let me and then had to let go of her hand and leave her. The nurse assured me Savannah could hear me and encouraged me to tell her I loved her and would see her soon. I was her husband, after all, and those were the things I should be saying.

I kissed her hand and leaned down near her ear and told her she was so brave and I would be right here when she got done. Then I kissed her and whispered I loved her. It wasn't just for the nurse's benefit, either. I loved her. I knew it the moment I vowed my heart to her on Saturday that going back to the way it was a few months ago was going to rip my heart out.

I doubted when she woke up, she would remember the words, but there was always a chance. I could pass it off as drug-induced if I wanted to, but I wouldn't. If she says something about it, I'll be honest with her, because telling someone you love them shouldn't be a lie, ever.

"Mr. Kiss?" a voice asked and I sat up quickly when I saw the scrubs clad figure. It was the same nurse that had taken her to the operating room.

"Yes," I answered quickly.

"Savannah is out of surgery now and in recovery. She did wonderfully. Dr. Kent needs to talk to you about the surgery. If you come with me, I'll take you to a private waiting room," she explained.

I stood and realized the long hours of sitting

had left my back sore and achy. “Is she doing okay? Did the surgery go well?” I asked the nurse, picking up my phone.

She put her hand on my arm. “She’s doing okay in recovery. I can’t tell you anything more than that, but Dr. Kent will. I know you’re anxious, but she’s a real trooper.”

I nodded and followed her down a short hallway to a small room with four chairs and a wooden table. She left me there alone and as soon as she disappeared, I sank into the closest chair and put my head in my hands.

She’s doing okay, I told myself.

Surgery is done and now she can recover and get back to her life. She can finally put Günther behind her.

For some reason, those words weren’t comforting to my soul the way they should have been. Instead, they invoked even more anxiety in my heart.

“Noel,” Dr. Kent spoke and I glanced up at the man dressed in scrubs, his hair covered with a surgical hat.

“Hello, Dr. Kent. How is she?” I asked without preamble and he sat in the chair across from me.

“The surgery went very well. What I found was an aneurysm of the carotid plexus, which runs along the carotid artery,” he explained, showing me a diagram on his computer.

“This outpouching was compressing the facial nerve, which was causing the paralysis. It was also compressing the trigeminal nerve, which was causing the spasms and shearing pain." He outlined the areas as he spoke, so I was able to understand it easily.

"How did that happen? The outpouching thing?" I asked.

He set the computer down. "It probably happened from the trauma when she was punched." He motioned in a circle by his eye. "We saw evidence of a healed orbital fracture on imaging, and during the surgery. The nerves in the face are all consolidated in this area and then branch out from there. If trauma occurs to that area, then the disruption in the nerves also branch out from there."

I nodded my understanding and tried to stay calm. "Were you able to remove the problem and fix her face?"

He sighed heavily and I had a sinking feeling in my gut. "I was able to repair the outpouching and relieve the pressure on the part of the nerve that controls the eye. Her eye returned to normal once we decompressed it."

"But?" I asked, knowing in my gut there was one.

"But the nerve that controls her lips and cheek wasn't so cooperative."

"What does that mean?" I asked slowly.

"We test the nerves as we go during surgery and the trigeminal nerve branch that was causing the spasms was damaged and misfiring, so to say, which is why she kept having the spasms."

"So, she's still going to have the spasms?"

"No," he rubbed a hand over his face. "She's probably not going to feel anything in her face on that side from about here to here." He motioned from below his cheekbone to just below his bottom lip.

"She won't be able to smile or anything?" I asked in shock.

He shook his head. "I don't think so. Not on that side. I had to sacrifice the nerve to remove the outpouching and repair the carotid. I'm sorry, I had to choose between the eye or the cheek. I'm always going to preserve vision."

I ran my hands through my hair. "No, I understand, but you mean she won't be able to feel her face at all, ever again?" I asked, picturing my hand on her face and her not knowing I was there for her.

"The chances are good that's the case, Noel. She won't feel much from about her ear to below her lip. The trigeminal nerve is very complicated because it divides into three branches that cover most of the face. It's also the nerve that was responsible for her facial spasms and burning pain. If I didn't sacrifice the nerve, she would continue to have pain and would require medication daily to control it. By doing what I did, she won't have to suffer from the pain and spasms anymore, but she also won't have feeling or function, so it's a catch 22. There's always the chance the nerve could regenerate. If that happens, she could regain normal facial function and have no pain. It could also mean the pain will return and she will need medication or a second procedure."

My hands were shaking I was so upset. "You're telling me she is going to have to deal with this for the rest of her life?"

"I'm afraid that's the situation as it stands right now. I've done what I can to remove the compression that was pressing on the nerves, but unfortunately, the damage has been done. She will need close follow-up as she heals to make sure the pain doesn't recur."

"I'm sorry, I wasn't expecting this." I sighed. "My emotions are all over the place."

"Noel, it's never easy when dealing with the direct result of domestic abuse. I want you to know we've done everything we can for Savannah."

"Does she know?" I asked.

He shook his head. "No, she's still waking up from the anesthesia in the recovery room. We need to break the news to her slowly. When she wakes up, she will be able to see again, so I want you to be really encouraging about how great that is." He paused and I nodded my agreement. "She may wonder why her face is numb before I get in there to see her tomorrow. The nurses will tell her it's from the surgery and you can reinforce that as well. Once she's clearheaded tomorrow, I will come in and talk with you both about what we did, and what she can expect. I want her to see the good things that have come from this before she hears the rest. She loves you and trusts you, so I think it would be wise if you stay close tonight and don't leave her."

"I just can't believe she is going to have to deal with this for the rest of her life because of him," I ground out, angry at the situation.

"She'll get through it with your help. I know you married her so she would have insurance. That's more than a lot of men would do."

I stared at him, shaking my head vehemently and wondering if he saw through our façade. "No, I didn't marry her just because of that."

He held his hand up. "I'm sorry, I didn't mean to insult you. What I meant was, I know you got married quicker than you would have if this hadn't come up. I think that says a lot about your character. You could have walked away, but instead, you ran straight into the fire to protect her. Savannah told us how much she loves you. I know you will get through this together."

I cleared my throat. "She told you how much she loves me?"

Dr. Kent laughed and stood up. "Don't worry, she didn't tell any secrets. It's not uncommon for patients to let their emotions take hold of them when under sedation. Now, if you'll excuse me, I'm going to go dictate this report and call Snow."

"You're going to call Snow?" I asked, surprised.

"She's the referring physician, so it's common courtesy, but she's also my friend. Savannah is like a sister to her, and I don't want her worrying. I don't want to put her baby's health at risk. I also don't want her to come down here when she's pregnant. I will call her and tell her in specific detail what I did. I'll assure her Savannah will be home in a few days. I'm sure she'll call you once we're through."

"Thank you, Dr. Kent. I appreciate everything you have done to help Savannah." I shook his hand again and he nodded, then stopped at the door without turning around.

"Did she press charges?" he asked, his voice hushed.

"No, she was too afraid of him."

"So, he could be doing this to another woman," he spat angrily.

I shifted uncomfortably. "Not anymore. Snow called me this morning. Apparently, he was killed in a logging accident yesterday. Savannah doesn't even know yet."

He turned and smiled, though I could tell it was sardonically. "Savannah has gone through hell because of him, and I hope that is where his soul goes. Saying that may send me there as well, but I've seen so many women destroyed by a man like him in my career. Days like today, it's hard to come to work. If you can avoid mentioning his death to Savannah for a few days, that would be wise. Let her get back on an even keel before you knock her off balance again."

"Won't be a problem, Dr. Kent," I assured him. "I have no intention of telling her until she's back home."

He tapped the doorjamb and headed down the hallway. I sat back down and let out a heavy breath. I had only a short time to get my own emotions under control before they would take me to her room and I would need to be her rock. How could I do that when he just told me she loves me? I shook my head. It was probably the drugs talking. He admitted himself that sedation can make patients emotional. Dr. Kent stopped in the hallway and spoke with a nurse before pointing toward me in the room. I stood up and went to the door as the nurse approached.

"Noel Kiss?" she asked, and I nodded mutely. "Would you come with me?"

"Why?" I asked, already trying to catch up with her as she headed back down the hallway at a fast pace.

"I'm one of the nurses in the recovery area. Your wife is having a tough time waking up from the anesthesia. Her blood pressure and pulse are spiking and she's extremely agitated. We don't usually bring the family back to recovery, but you may be the only one who can calm her. She keeps calling for you." She pushed a door open and I followed her through, my mind still racing to process the information Dr. Kent gave me.

I reached out and took the nurse by the arm, stopping her for a moment. "Is she going to be okay?"

"If you can calm her down, she'll be fine. If she doesn't improve her vitals soon, we may have to send her to the ICU, and we want to avoid doing that," she explained, holding the curtain back.

My wife lay on the bed, her tiny frame engulfed by blankets, tubes, and wires. She was crying softly when I approached the bed.

"I'm here, angel. It's okay. Surgery is all over," I whispered, taking her hand carefully because of all the tubes in it.

I wiped away a tear from her cheek and noticed how nicely her eye closed now. Her face was relaxed and she looked so peaceful. Then I saw the missing piece of hair behind her ear and the bandage almost a foot long.

A chair touched my thighs and I sat immediately, my knees going weak with the thought of the pain she must have been in.

"Noel," she whispered, her mouth dry and her tongue darting out to wet her lips.

"I'm here, honey. The surgery went very well. Your eye looks normal again, angel. You're so beautiful," I whispered, kissing her eye.

She squeezed my hand and the nurse gave me a thumbs-up as she checked the monitor.

Savannah struggled to sit up and I rubbed her shoulder, holding her down. "I know you're disoriented and scared right now, but you need to stay down a little while longer. Let the medicine wear off, so you feel better. You're going to be dizzy, so take it easy. Are you in pain?" I asked, laying my head just inches from her pillow.

"No, no pain," she croaked. "I'm scared."

I leaned forward and kissed her lips. "Don't be scared. Everything is done and over now. I'm not going to leave. I'll be right here."

"You're going to leave," she whispered. "Someday, you're going to leave, and I'll be alone. I love you so much, Noel. Please don't leave me alone."

She was crying again, and I slipped one arm under her and the other around her to hug her to me carefully. "I'm not going anywhere, Savannah. Shh, just sleep and let the medicine wear off."

I held her next to me until the nurse tapped my shoulder and pointed to the blood pressure cuff. I released her enough for it to inflate and waited for it to deflate. She smiled when the reading came up on the screen. I sat back down in the chair but made sure to keep both hands on Savannah at all times.

She loves me. It wasn't the drugs talking. She was scared I was going to leave, that was so real the room throbbed with it. The question is, what do we do now?

Chapter Thirteen

Savannah

I rolled over carefully onto my back and stared up at the ceiling. The bandage behind my ear was thick and bulky and kept my head from touching the pillow on that side. I blinked a few times and felt my lid open and close like it used to. I let out a sigh of relief. My eye was working again. I heard shifting and glanced to my right to see Noel next to the bed. His eyes were sleepy and his clothes rumpled.

"You're still here," I sighed, and he brushed some hair off my face.

"Of course, I am. I told you I wouldn't leave you. Are you okay? Do I need to call a nurse?" he asked nervously.

I held his hand tightly. "No. I think the drugs just finally cleared my system and I woke up clear-headed. My eye works," I explained, touching my eye and then my face.

He pulled my hand down into his as he leaned over the bed. "Yes, Dr. Kent was able to relieve the compression. He said your eye went right back to normal when they released the nerve."

"That's good. I don't remember much," I admitted and he chuckled a little, pulling the chair closer to my bed and sitting down.

"You aren't supposed to remember much, that's the point. The important thing is you're feeling better. Do you remember talking to Snow?" he asked and I nodded carefully.

"I remember that and a few other things. She was so worried. I feel terrible making her worry so much when she's pregnant. She shouldn't be so worried about me, I'll be fine."

"She loves you. That's why she worries."

"Are you worried, too? You said you love me," I pointed out and then let my eyes close. "I'm sorry. I guess my mind isn't as clear as I thought it was."

He held my hand and rubbed the top with his thumb. "I guess you do remember a few things," he joked and I stared at him, his five o'clock shadow darkening his chin, and his eyes tired. I was going to speak, but he stopped me with his finger on my lips.

"Yes, I'm worried, but less now than I while you were in recovery. When they said you weren't doing well, I was scared to death. When I was the one to comfort and calm you, I felt like the most important person in the world to you. I told you I love you because I do. I know that might be a little bit scary right now, but it's the truth. I like to be honest and to be completely honest, I would have to tell you I've been in love with you since I first met you. You're probably the reason I left this life in Rochester behind and moved to Snowberry. Something inside my heart told me I needed to be near you, even if my head didn't know why yet. When I slipped the ring on your finger Saturday, it didn't feel like a sham to me. It was real. It felt like I always thought getting married would feel. It was wonderful, nerve-racking, and so amazing to feel that much love for one person when I pledged myself to you."

I looked down at the ring on my finger still covered in tape. They asked me to take it off, but I didn't want to, so instead, they taped it on so it wouldn't come off in surgery. I held my hand up and showed him the ring. "I didn't want to take it off this morning before surgery. When I feel it on my finger, I feel your love, even though that's not what I let myself believe it is. They taped it on so it wouldn't fall off."

He smiled and took my hand to peel the paper tape off carefully. "That looks much better."

I looked down at the ring and back to him. "I think I told you I loved you and begged you not to leave me at some point?"

He chuckled a little and rubbed my thigh. "It's okay, you were out of sorts and under the influence."

"I was out of sorts, but I knew you were in the room before you had even said anything. I felt it in here," I said, pointing to my chest and my hand encountered my necklace.

His hand covered mine. "I put it back on when

they brought you up here," he explained. "I know you didn't want to take that off, either. Your hand kept going to your chest like you were searching for it. The nurse said it was okay for it to be on."

"It's my angel. I kept searching for it because I was searching for you, I think. When I feel it, I feel you and I know I'm going to be all right," I explained feebly. "What I said in the recovery room, well, I know it wasn't a perfect time to say it, but it was certainly the most honest I've ever been. I love you, Noel. I don't remember when it happened. It's like I always have," I trailed off, shrugging.

He sighed and ducked his head, staring at the floor for a long time. His hand held mine and I finally whispered his name. When he looked up, he was crying, the tears rolling down his cheeks. He laughed a little and shrugged. "I'm sorry if I upset you." I shifted to my side to face him.

"No, you didn't upset me. Just the opposite. My heart burst open hearing you say you love me. I don't know where all of this will lead us, but I do know that I love you and I want to be with you. It's enough for me to know you love me too. All the rest can wait," he assured me, stroking my face. He leaned in and kissed my lips softly, barely putting any pressure on them at all before he sat back in the chair.

"Is that all I get?" I asked, laughing a little.

"For now, yes. I don't want to irritate your face."

"Do they have a mirror in here? I would like to

look at myself," I said, and he froze.

"Only in the bathroom, but no getting up tonight, they said."

"Where's my phone? I'll use my camera," I said, searching around my bed and finally spotting it on the dresser. He picked it up and held it in his hand, shaking his head.

"Not a good idea tonight, Savannah. Just rest. You're absolutely gorgeous, that's all you need to know," he promised.

"My face is numb and doesn't move right, Noel. I'm not dumb. I just want to see," I said forcefully.

"The doctor said that's from the surgery, the numbness, I mean." He motioned at his face again and I held my hand out for my phone.

He sighed and put it in my open palm. I turned it on and flipped the camera around, inspecting my face. Both my eyes looked right. They both pointed in the right direction and my lids opened and closed like they always did. My cheek and lip drooped slightly and I touched the cheek. The sensation was the same as when the dentist numbs your mouth before he fills a cavity. "My face isn't pulled up all grotesquely," I whispered.

"No, it's not. You look natural and comfortable now. Dr. Kent said there was a bundle of nerves compressing the big nerve in your face, that's why you had the pain and spasms. He fixed all of that. He promised to come by in the morning and explain everything," Noel explained, trying to take the phone, but I wouldn't let go.

"No, something's wrong. My face shouldn't be numb. The incision hurts and I can feel that." I felt around my eye and my chin. "I can feel my eye and my chin, but not here." I showed him. "Why can't I feel just that part?" I held the phone closer to my face and tried to make my face move up by smiling, but only the left side worked. "We need to call the nurse, something is wrong," I said frantically.

The phone disappeared from my hand and he shook his head. "Nothing is wrong. There's a lot to talk about, but it can wait until morning when Dr. Kent comes in. Let's rest now," he encouraged, trying to tuck me in.

I grabbed his arms until he was still. "Tell me the truth, Noel. I can see it in your eyes," I begged him.

He came around the other side of the bed and slipped in next to me, taking me in his arms. "You don't have any pain here?" he asked, rubbing his thumb over my cheekbone."

"None, everything is gone. It's all gone," I whispered.

"Not everything. You can see out of your eye again and that's very important."

I could tell he was holding something back as he kissed my temple.

"He had to sever the nerve, didn't he?" I asked. He stiffened and that was enough of an answer for me. I had the truth now, and nothing was going to be the same.

"He said the damage was so great he had to

make a decision. When it comes down to preserving vision, he always has to take that road."

I sighed, resting my head on his chest. "What else did he say?" I finally asked.

He gave a resigned sigh as though he knew he wouldn't be able to lie to me any longer. "Dr. Kent really wanted to talk to you about it tomorrow when the drugs are out of your system."

"Now, please." I started crying and the tears leaked from my eyes and wet his shirt.

"The nerve was damaged, sweetheart. That was causing the spasms and the pain. By sacrificing the nerve, he could save your eye, and hopefully, keep the pain at bay for the rest of your life."

"Hopefully?" I whimpered.

"He said there's a small chance it could grow back, and if it does, it might cause you no problems, or the pain could come back. You will have to keep watch of it, but I'm sure Snow won't have it any other way."

"Oh, my gosh, he got his wish," I choked out, the truth hitting me square in the gut.

"What wish, honey?" Noel asked patiently.

"Günther. While I was writhing in pain on the floor after he punched me, he said he wished he could punish me every day for the rest of my life. I guess he got his wish."

He sat up and held my chin in his hand. "No, Savannah, you can't think that way."

I put my hand over my mouth and saw it shaking. The reality of the situation was setting in and

I could hardly bear it. "He gets to walk around free to do whatever he wants while I suffer. How is that fair?" Before he could answer, the truth hit me. What if someone else had to suffer because I didn't stop him? I put my hand on my head. "I should have pressed charges, but I was scared of him. What if he's doing this to some other woman?"

"He's not." He nodded assuredly and I took his hand.

"You don't know that! Can I still press charges? Would Dr. Kent testify?" I asked questions as fast as my brain thought of them.

He shook me gently and I stopped talking long enough to look at him.

"Savannah, Günther is dead. Snow called me earlier today. He was killed in a logging accident yesterday."

"What?" I asked. The room started spinning and there were stars in my vision. I grabbed onto him and he laid me back on the pillows while he talked to me softly.

"I'm going to call the nurse and have her give you something for the dizziness." He grabbed the call button.

"Just don't leave me," I cried, the nausea building in my chest.

"I'm not going anywhere, sweetheart. I'm staying right here," he promised.

The darkness was closing in and I curled myself into a ball and lay against him. I succumbed to the darkness and let myself believe that was true.

"Hi, Snow." I leaned against the backdoor and watched my friend wheel up the ramp.

"I had to come over to see you," she explained. "No one would let me go to Rochester."

I stepped out onto the ramp and held the door so she could wheel through. "I'm glad they didn't let you come down, not in your condition. Besides, I'm fine, and I've only been gone a few days."

She took my hand, giving me the once over. "I'm pregnant, it's not a condition, and you've been gone for six days, three of which you spent in a hospital bed while I was stuck here. Where's Noel?"

I pointed towards the kitchen. "He went to the store. We got home late last night and forgot there was no food in the house."

She pulled me along into the living room and hoisted herself onto the couch. She patted the spot next to her and waited for me to sit. I sat next to her and her tiny arms enveloped me. I felt just like I used to feel years ago when I needed her comfort. I was safe. The same way I felt in Noel's arms, even if I don't like to admit it.

"How are you handling everything?" she whisper-asked into my ear.

I laid my head over her shoulder and sighed. "I'm okay. Better now that you're here."

She leaned back against the couch and kept hold of my hand. "Dr. Kent kept me updated, but I had to see you. Talking to you on the phone isn't the same."

I nodded. "I missed you, too. Noel took good care of me, though, so stop worrying."

She glanced down at my hands and then back up to my face, her eyes focused on my cheek. I took her hand and laid it against it. "You can touch it. I can't feel anything."

She moved her hand to the corner of my eye and then turned my head slowly, inspecting the incision behind my ear. "Oh, Savan, I'm so sorry."

Her hand fell and I tried to smile, though my façade was cracking. "It looks worse than it is. I barely notice it."

"I'm sorry for all of this. I wish like mad I had been a better sister and done something to keep you from staying with him. I should have done more," she cried, her voice cracking and tears rolling down her face.

I grabbed a tissue off the coffee table and pressed it into her hand. "Snow, you have to stop. You can't blame yourself for this. You warned me and I chose not to listen, that's on me." I rested my hand on her little belly and raised my brow at her. "Please stop worrying. I don't want anything to happen to you or Lila Jo."

Snow sighed out the name in her own voice, and it wasn't a question as much as a statement. "Lila Jo, I haven't heard that in a long time."

I smiled, at least half my face did. "I think a lot about Grandma Jo. I see so much of Jo in Sunny. I think about our new little girl and when I do, I call her Lila Jo. I don't know why."

"Grandma loved this house, and she loved you, that's probably why." Snow patted my hand on her belly.

I leaned my head back against the couch. "Sometimes, I wish I could go back to those days before everything bad happened."

"That's not how life works I'm afraid, pretty lady." She laughed and I nodded.

"I know. Is it bad that I take great comfort in knowing that Günther can't hurt another woman? Does it make me a bad person to be relieved he's dead?" I asked, rolling the ring around on my finger.

"Noel told you," she sighed.

"Of course, he told me. He kind of had to. I decided while on drugs, I was going to press charges." I snorted and she tilted her head back to copy me, a smile on her face.

"That might have been fun to see." She punched me lightly. "To answer your question, no, it doesn't make you a terrible person to feel that way. I would say it's natural. You've feared him for a very long time, and now you don't have to. Now you can finally enjoy your new life with Noel."

My chin trembled and I knew I was going to fall apart at just the mention of his name. I stood quickly, nearly tipping over onto the coffee table.

Snow grabbed me and pulled me back down to the couch. "Savan, you have to be careful when you get up. Are you okay?"

"No, I'm not okay," I cried, my heart tearing in two as I thought about Noel and how I wouldn't have a new life with him.

Snow gazed at me intently. "Tell me what's going on. Is it your face or your heart?"

"It's my life. I'm such a disaster," I moaned and she pulled me over to lay my head on her lap.

"I'm here to listen," she soothed, rubbing my arm.

For a moment, I almost told her, but then I didn't. "I'll be okay, don't worry," I promised. I wouldn't convince her, but maybe I could convince myself.

"You know you can tell me anything," she prodded, squeezing my arm.

"I just want life to be normal again. I want to go to my shop and smell the flowers. I want to not worry about losing the house or the business or Noel," I whispered.

"Why would you lose Noel, honey?"

She was rubbing my arm and the rhythm was making me sleepy. "I have to let him go, Snow. I can't expect him to stay married to me with my face like it is."

Her hand stopped moving. "Did Noel ask for a divorce?"

"No, he's been nothing but wonderful to me," I said sadly.

"I'm confused then. Why do you have to let him go? He married you when your face was in worse shape than it is now," she pointed out.

"He married me thinking my face would go back to normal after the surgery. Instead, I look like this." I motioned to my face. "Can you imagine our family pictures? Years later, our kids would say, "Mom was such a sourpuss, why did Dad stay with her?"

"Savannah, you're being a little hard on yourself here," Snow reasoned. "Noel doesn't love you because one side of your face doesn't move the same as the other. He loves you for you."

I didn't answer her, just laid on her lap until my eyes were too heavy to keep open.

Noel

The grocery bags were heavy and I set them on the stoop and tried the door. It was still locked, so I dug my keys out and unlocked the front door. Snow's van was in the driveway, as I knew it would be, so I wondered what they were doing. I picked up the bags again and set them inside the door and pulled off my gloves. Snow waved at me from the couch, where she sat with Savannah on her lap, asleep.

I waved and mouthed *hi*, then pulled my coat off and hung it up on the rack. I shucked my shoes and tiptoed to the couch. *"I'll take her to bed,"* I mouthed and Snow nodded, lifting her hand off her arm.

I slid my hands under her and twisted her up and into my arms, being careful of the incision on the back of her head. She startled awake for a moment and when she saw me, drifted back to sleep. I laid her in our bed and pulled the covers up around her, turning the lights off and pulling the door.

When I got back to the living room, I found Snow in the kitchen making tea. I brought the bags over from the front door and started unloading them.

"Nice to see you, Snow." I smiled and she didn't even answer me, just sighed a little. "Did something happen?" I asked, her body language telling me something was wrong. "Are you sick? Should I call Dully?"

She held her hand out and shook her head. "No, I'm just fine. I'm worried about Savannah, though."

She dunked her teabag up and down incessantly while I loaded the fridge. Finally, I turned to the counter to face her. "She's doing okay. Even Dr. Kent says she's ahead of most people at this stage of the game."

Snow sipped her tea. "That's not what I'm worried about. She told me a bit ago she has to let you go. She said she can't ask you to stay with her now that her face will never be normal." She motioned at her cheek and then let her hand fall.

"Oh, boy," I sighed.

I took hold of the back of MAC and rolled her

into the living room where we could talk out of earshot of the bedroom.

"She told me her life is a disaster and she can't stop worrying about losing the house, the business, and you. The next breath she told me she has to let you go because it isn't fair to ask you to stay. Maybe it's just the medication making her feel anxious. She wasn't making a lot of sense." Snow set her tea on the table and I sighed again.

"I think the medication is making it hard for her to express herself, but she's telling the truth. Honestly, I'm afraid to lose her, too, but I know it's coming." I stopped and stared at Snow, not sure how much she even knew about the situation. "Did she tell you she was a month away from foreclosure on the house?"

Snow's eyes grew wide. "No! What, wait, no, how can that be?"

"She said after Günther left, she thought she could afford the house and the business mortgage together, but she was sinking fast. I agreed to move in here and pay half the house mortgage, so she could stay."

Snow put her head in her hand. "I wish she had said something. I would have helped her."

I smiled and patted her leg. "I know you would have, but she really has this thing about asking for help." I rolled my eyes a little, and Snow snorted.

"You don't say?"

"So how serious is this? Is she going to lose the business?" Snow asked, concerned.

"No, she would have let the house go before she let the business go, but I know how much she loves this house."

She got a faraway look in her eye. "Yeah, my Grandma Jo was good to her. They were kindred spirits. I wouldn't have let her lose the house, but I'm glad you were able to help. What I can't figure out is why she's afraid to lose you, yet says she has to let you go."

I picked up my soda and took a long swallow. "It's really a complicated, twisted mess, Snow," I finally admitted. "I don't even know where to start."

"How about at the beginning," she suggested and I leaned forward.

"That would be when I first saw her at Deccy's wedding. She reminded me of a rose. She started out all closed up and hiding, but the more I got her to talk, the more her petals opened up. When she had the first attack, it ripped my guts out. I shouldn't have had that kind of reaction toward someone I just met, but in that instant, I would have taken it all on me to spare her. After I left on Christmas Day, I couldn't get her out of my head. The way she smelled, the way she laughed, but more than that was the underlying way she expressed her sadness and fear. I don't know, but something made me come back here and toss the rest of my life aside. I didn't know why."

"Sounds a little like something we call love," she teased.

"Maybe, at least smitten, but I don't know if you understand how much I didn't have a choice. I had no control. It was like I was doing all these things that didn't make sense, but I was driven by a force I couldn't see. Once I got here, I found out why."

"You asked her to marry you pretty quickly, so you must have known deep down that was what you wanted," Snow pointed out, sipping her tea again.

"No, I didn't. I moved in with her intending to help with the mortgage while I got the café up and running. I knew I needed to be close to her, so I could help her with the pain, but I didn't know why until one night."

"Really, Noel, I don't need to hear personal things that should stay between you and Savan." She choked on her tea a little with her eyes wide.

I chuckled. "No, that's not what I'm talking about. We haven't even…" I shifted uncomfortably and she leaned forward.

"Noel? Do you mean you haven't consummated the marriage?"

I shook my head and set my soda down, feeling the red flush to my cheeks. "Like I said, it's a twisted mess."

"I suddenly feel like I'm missing a big part of the picture. What were you talking about one night then, if it wasn't that kind of night?"

"It was the night of Deccy's reception. We got home, and she had a terrible attack." I motioned at my face and she nodded. "I was up half the night keeping her comfortable and trying to give her relief by keeping the icepack cold while she slept. I finally drifted to sleep early in the morning and had a dream." I stopped and she gave me the keep going motion with her hands.

"What kind of dream?" she prodded.

"I feel a little ridiculous talking about this," I told her, getting up and checking down the hallway. The door to the bedroom was still as I'd left it and Savannah was curled up on the bed.

I paced the room, too keyed up to sit. "I fell asleep trying to figure out how to get her the treatment she needed, so the pain would end. In the dream, I was holding a job fair and the only person who came was you."

"Me?" she asked perplexed.

"I told you it sounds ridiculous," I groaned.

"I didn't say it was ridiculous. I was just making sure I heard you right. Carry on," she motioned.

"Long story short, you told me to marry Savannah. If I married her, then I could put her on my insurance," I explained quickly. "I shouldn't be telling you this, you're a doctor."

She folded her hands over her lap. "I am a doctor, but more than that, I'm her best friend. She's the closest thing I've got to a sister, Noel. If you hadn't come along, we were going to figure out a way to pay the premiums or somehow get her the surgery, so I'm not judging you. Don't think I am.

You're basically telling me this was a marriage of convenience, so Savannah had insurance."

I nodded. "It was, in the beginning, but now I know I love her, and I can't go through with the divorce."

Snow was quiet for a long time, sipping her tea with her eyes closed. I leaned against the wall and stared out the window, trying to make sense of all the things running through my tired mind.

"What did I tell you to do in the dream, Noel? After the marrying her part, anyway," she finally asked.

"That's just the thing, you didn't!" I exclaimed, throwing my arms up at the sky. "You didn't tell me anything other than to marry her. When I asked you what if Savannah said no, your response was *what if she says yes?* That was it."

"That's a good question, what if she said yes? Was her answer the most important part of the whole thing? If she said yes, did that mean Savannah found someone she could trust again?" she pondered, a little too accepting of the situation in my opinion.

"Snow, I have no idea. What does that have to do with anything?" I asked, exasperated and exhausted.

"Actually, everything. When Savannah told me she was getting married, I didn't suspect it was for any reason other than love. I like to think I'm not the kind of person who has her head in the clouds. I'm a scientific and fact-based person who can read people's true feelings even when they think they're fooling me. What I saw in both of your eyes when you told me individually you were getting married, was love. Was there hesitation? Yes, I read that, but it made sense to me that you were nervous. You hadn't known each other very long when you got engaged, and Savannah was in the middle of a crisis. But when I looked in your eyes, I could see you loved her. You wanted to take her pain away. When Savannah looked at you, I could see how much she loved you, how much she needed you to take her pain away."

"She told Dr. Kent and all the nurses how much she loves me, but she was under heavy sedation," I tried to reason. "Now she's trying to push me away. I just don't know what to do."

"I do," she said, "it's obvious."

"Could you share with those of us who are a little obtuse?"

"You love her."

"That's it?" I asked my hand on my hip.

She held her hand out. "That's it. I assume you've told her that you love her?"

"Multiple times," I assured her. "She told me she loves me, but she doesn't trust me. I have to be there to hold her all night, or she doesn't sleep, but in the light of day, she closes the petals up and won't let me in. If I try to kiss her during the day, she turns away, but at night I can kiss her with no hesitation. I wish she would tell me how she's feeling."

"I'm not a psychologist, but I do know Savannah. I'm pretty sure I have it figured out now. She expected to go into this surgery and come back out her normal self, with her face whole and her life back in perfect order. She loves everything to be in perfect order. Has she told you about her childhood?" She paused and I nodded. "If she feels like her life is spinning out of control, her only way to deal with it is to clam up, or in your words, close her petals. And I like that, by the way, I think you know her far better than she gives you credit for." She smiled and I nodded, a little embarrassed. "Anyway, Savannah has never known real, genuine, meaningful love from a man, but then she meets you. You jump in with both feet and marry her when she's not perfect. She's a mess of pain, anger, and hurt, but you don't care. Savannah tells herself when she's healthy again, she can handle you leaving and go on with her life, even though she already loves you desperately. When she wakes up from surgery, she finds out she will never have that normal, orderly life again. Her face will never look the same, and suddenly, she can't deal with the idea of letting you go. She feels like she's being punished for being stupid..."

I jumped in. "Wait, did she tell you that? Did she use those words?" I asked angrily.

Snow held her hands out. "Settle down, Noel. I'm not calling her stupid. She does enough of that herself. I was just quoting her."

I rubbed a hand over my face. "I'm sorry, I hate

it when she calls herself stupid. She does it all the time like if she degrades herself, I'll accept her words and leave because she isn't smart enough to be with me."

Snow nodded. "Oh, yes, that was the first two years of our relationship. When she told me this was punishment for being stupid and marrying Günther, I told her that being stuck in a wheelchair is punishment for my parents being stupid and living in the Congo. She didn't like that so much."

I laughed softly. "No, I bet she didn't. She's fiercely protective of you."

"Well, you haven't seen fierce protection. She's been hurt enough in this life and she deserves happiness. I'm going to ask you this once, and you better answer me honestly." She waited and I put my hands up, agreeing. "Do you want to be with her? Do you want to make a life with her, and love that woman the way she deserves to be loved, even if her face isn't perfect?" She was jabbing her finger towards the bedroom with every word.

I reached out and lowered her arm to her side. "I'm still here, aren't I? I'm not going anywhere, Snow. I just need to figure out how to convince her of that."

Snow transferred back into MAC and buckled the seatbelt. "The only advice I can give you is to love her. Maybe that's all she needs. For the record, I'm not going to tell anyone you married her, so she had insurance because I don't believe for a second that by Saturday night, that was the only reason you were standing there, right?"

I shook my head. "No, I was standing there because I loved her."

"Noel?" I heard my name from down the hall. It was soft, but I could hear the hesitation in her voice. I held my finger up to Snow, but didn't move. My name came again, more frantic this time, as though she thought I was gone.

I glanced at Snow but called out to her. "I'll be right there, sweetheart. I'm right here."

"Do you hear her voice? She's afraid I've left, and I'm never coming back. Ask her about it, though, and she'll deny it." I gave Snow a hug. "Thanks for the words of advice and encouragement. I better go be with her before she gets too worked up."

Snow dropped her hands from my waist. "I'll lock the back door on my way out. Take care of my girl, and remember, she loves you, even if she doesn't know how to show it."

I waved goodbye and walked down the hallway to the bedroom. Savannah was curled up on her side, staring at the door. "I'm sorry for freaking out. Sometimes the medication makes me anxious and disoriented. Is Snow still here? I fell asleep on her."

I went around the other side of the bed and crawled up, wrapping my arms around her and resting my head on her pillow. "She just left to pick-up Sunny," I assured her, settling in. "You know how you feel when you think I'm not here?

When your heart starts beating fast and you can hardly breathe?" I asked, stroking her arm.

"Yeah, I don't like that feeling," she whimpered.

"Me either, but that's how I feel every minute of every day," I told her, kissing the spot below her incision that was closed with metal staples.

"Why?" She stiffened a little and I touched the pulse throbbing in her neck.

"Because I love you, and I can feel you pushing me away. When I think about not being here to hold you like this, my heart starts to race and I can't breathe."

"Why do you want to stay, Noel?" she asked desperately.

I pulled the covers over both of us and wrapped her in my arms. "Because I love you."

Chapter Fourteen

I glanced at Savannah sitting in the passenger seat of the car, staring out the window. It was now ten days since the surgery and we just left Rochester after seeing the doctor.

"Dr. Kent seemed happy with your progress," I said as I pulled out of Rochester onto Highway 14.

"I'm so happy to have those staples out of my head," she sighed. "I'm dying to wash my hair. Do you think Crow can do anything with this?" she asked, holding it up a little.

I smiled and flipped on the windshield wipers as light snow started falling. "I think Crow can do just about anything. What were you thinking?"

She shrugged. "I don't know, maybe just cut it all off to match the spot that's missing and let it regrow evenly."

"That makes sense to me." I didn't have it out of my mouth before I wondered if it was the wrong thing to say.

"Right, because why should it matter if I shave my head since I already look like this," she muttered, still staring out the window.

I bit my tongue to keep from saying anything.

The last week had been filled with the same kind of passive-aggressive comments and I refuted every one of them. Maybe I needed to change my tactic and go with her ideas. Show her she was beautiful regardless of her hair, face, or clothes.

"You could have Crow cut the back short and leave the front a little longer, so you can still pin flowers in your hair when you start back at the emporium," I suggested. "I know you like to wear a flower in your hair."

She turned and stared at me for a moment. "Do you think so?"

"I know so, and I think it might make you feel better to be able to keep doing that one small thing for yourself."

She nodded and went back to the window, staring at the falling flakes. "I'm sorry I've been a real pain lately. I can't catch up to my emotions half the time, and I'm not normally like that. I say things before I think, and think things I shouldn't."

I reached over and rubbed her thigh. "I think you have every right to be caught up in your emotions right now. You've had a lot to deal with and we all cope with it differently. You're doing a much better job at handling it than you think you are, too. I want you to know that."

She put her hand over mine. "I'm trying, but the pain has me so worn out, and now everything else."

I nodded, agreeing without words. The past week had also been punctuated with calls from insurance companies telling her she was still the beneficiary of Günther's insurance policies. She willingly signed the paperwork to transfer it over to her ex-mother-in-law, but it was something she wasn't expecting nor should have had to deal with. His service was yesterday and I took her to the emporium to do some paperwork just to get her mind off it. She could only work for a few hours at a time, but April was doing a great job of holding down the fort.

"April sure has been a godsend," I said, my voice loud in the quiet car.

"I don't know what we would do without her. Not only has she kept the emporium open, but she's also increased sales. If you hadn't already hired her, I might," she said, laughing.

"She's yours anytime you need her, sweetheart. I always share." I grinned, and she punched me lightly on the shoulder.

"Tell me something you've never told anyone else before." I glanced at her for a moment then back to the road.

"A deep dark secret, huh?" she asked, and I nodded. She tapped her chin a few times. "I write poetry."

I raised one brow without taking my eyes off the road. "I wasn't expecting poetry. What kind?"

"There are kinds of poetry?" she questioned, and I could tell she was sincere.

"Yes, there are lots of kinds of poetry. Blank verse, haiku, ballad poems, prose."

She shrugged again. "I told you I'm not very smart, but you didn't believe me."

"I don't think I said anything about you being dumb, did I?" I threw back, angry that she always found a way to put herself down.

She was quiet for a moment. "Well, I don't know what kind they are, I guess. I started writing when I was very young. Anything could spark a poem; a bird, a tree, even a clean bed. I always said I wasn't smart enough to write an entire book."

"How many poems do you think you've written over the years?"

"Oh, thousands, for sure. Sometimes, I write one or two a day. Say, for instance, a guy wants to send flowers to his girlfriend but doesn't know what to say. Well, I'll write something flowery and romantic. If I'm sending flowers to someone in the hospital, I'll write a get-well poem. You get it."

"I do get it. You use this secret talent of yours and give all the credit to everyone else. You say you're too dumb to write a whole book, but if you had all those poems in one place, you'd have a book. Ever thought of that?"

"No, because I do it as a way to release my feelings and cope with what might be stressing me out. What about you? What's your darkest secret that you've never told anyone?"

"Late at night, I lay bare, my soul devoid of life. I close my eyes and wait. Wait. Wait. After an eternity, I am carried off to a far-away land. There to learn another way to show you my love with a poet's hand," I trailed off, and the car was silent other than the sound of her breathing.

"That was beautiful. Did you write that?" she asked.

"Guilty as charged." I glanced at her and saw the look of admiration on her face. "I write poetry, too. Even Deccy doesn't know. How weird is it that we both write poetry? Tell me one of yours."

"Okay, um, I've never actually said them out loud, so it might sound dumb." I leveled one eye at her, and she held up her hands. "Sorry. This is one I wrote on Christmas morning. The sun has stolen my cloak of darkness and left me exposed, splayed out and raw. Just one look and you will see the truth I hide in my deepest depths of red. I am four and swinging on a swing. I am six and digging for a shell. I am ten and sitting by myself. I am twelve and looking for a hand. I am many. I am few. I am all of you."

"Incredible," I breathed. "You should read at a poetry slam. Seriously, you're that good." She tossed her hand at me in disregard, but I could see she was pleased. "You wrote that just this past Christmas morning?"

"Oh, yeah, I was feeling pretty exposed that morning with you in my house and me, well, me."

"You, wonderful you, you mean," I corrected her and she looked away shyly.

The snow was coming down harder the closer we got to Snowberry and it was difficult to see the road in front of me. I fell silent as I watched the road between the swipes of the windshield wipers.

I could feel the tires slipping a little under us and in a truck this size with four-wheel drive, that shouldn't happen. If the tires were slipping, that told me one thing, ice. I couldn't lose control of the truck with her in it. Dr. Kent said we had to be very careful not to knock her head or face over the next few months as she healed. If we disturbed the nerves, we could have a new problem on our hands.

It was growing dark to add to my worries, and the headlights were barely cutting a path across the road in front of me. The backend started to slip toward the ditch and I corrected the wheel, finally getting control after fishtailing for a few seconds. I could see Savannah out of the corner of my eye. She was holding onto the handle of the door tightly and her face was pinched.

I didn't take my hands off the wheel but tried to soothe her all the same. "Savannah, please relax. I'm going to get you home safely, I promise. Relax your face so you don't end up in pain, honey."

We had to be on the outskirts of Snowberry soon, and I prayed I could hold on a little longer to keep her safe. She was still holding onto the door, but her face had relaxed a little bit. She closed her eyes and was using the breathing techniques Snow had taught her. I didn't interrupt her, just let her carry on with what kept her calm.

After what felt like an eternity, I turned down the street toward home. The plows had come through once, and the driveway was filled with snow, but I was able to get the truck up over the mound and parked in front of the garage.

"Stay here, I'm going to shovel a path," I said, hopping down from the truck. I grabbed the shovel near the garage door and made a path from the truck to the front door. I shoveled off the steps and slipped when I hit a patch of ice.

The stairs and sidewalk were covered in ice, something the weathermen hadn't predicted. I picked my way back to the truck, trying to keep some snow packed on the sidewalk to help her in. I opened my door and motioned to her.

"Come out this way. It's really icy out and I don't want you to fall."

Once we made it up the steps to the house, I unlocked the door and helped her inside.

"Oh, I'm glad to be home. Thank you for driving me," she sighed, handing me her coat and slipping off her boots. I shrugged out of my winter gear and slipped my arms around her waist.

"You don't have to thank me, honey. There was no place else I was going to be today." I kissed her forehead.

"You have a business to run and I know you've been so busy with me you've been shirking your duties there."

She went to the fireplace and flicked on the switch, watching the fire until it filled the small room with a warm glow.

"First and foremost, I have a wife who needs

me, the business comes second. Big Eddie has everything under control and keeps me updated daily," I assured her from the kitchen where I turned some music on low then started the oven to bake a pizza. Going out wasn't an option, but after that drive, I wasn't interested in cooking, either.

She was still standing in the middle of the room when I came around the counter and took her hand. "Come dance with me," I crooned and she let me pull her into an embrace and sway in front of the fire. "You feel good in my arms," I whispered in her ear, kissing my way along the ridge near her incision until she reared back.

"Don't, Noel. Please," she begged, her body stiffening.

"Don't what?" I asked, confused.

"Don't kiss me there. Don't kiss me anywhere. When you kiss me, it makes me want to stay with you, and I can't stay with you." She wrenched out of my arms and ran behind the couch.

"I want you to stay with me, Savannah. Why can't you stay with me?" I asked for the tenth time in the last few days.

"You didn't ask for this, Noel. You didn't ask for a wife with a messed-up face. You're so kind, loving, and patient, and you deserve better than me. I'm used up, damaged, unrepairable," she cried.

"Savannah, no, stop." I took a step toward her, but she held up her hand.

"You can't deny it! The proof is staring you in the face, Noel. If you stay, you'll stare at my weird face day after day knowing some other man was the one to desecrate me. You'll have to worry about how to take care of me if it gets worse or comes back. You didn't sign up for that. I can't help that I fell in love with you, but I can keep you from making the biggest mistake of your life by staying. I would give you up a thousand times before I asked you to stay once." She was crying and her words slurred from her pain and anger.

I walked toward her slowly, my hands out. "Savannah, your face isn't damaged, your face is beautiful. I fell in love with who you are as a person, not what your face looks like. If your face changed again tomorrow, I wouldn't care. I love you because of who you are in your heart, not what you see in the mirror." I paused for a breath and she backed up toward the door, shaking her head.

"I love you, Noel, so much I have to let you go." She turned and fled from the room. The door to the bathroom slammed shut and the water in the shower turned on. I hung my head and shook it a little.

Maybe it was time for a little less talk and a lot more action.

Chapter Fifteen

The sun was shining and I walked behind the restaurant and up the new ramp where Eddie was working on the door frame and automatic door opener. "You guys are really moving along," I said, and he stopped hammering and looked up.

"Hey, boss, you betcha. You don't offer free pancakes and expect us not to get the job done, do ya?" He laughed, his belly shaking.

"The bad news is, we have to delay the opening, but the good news is, you will still get free pancakes because the reason is out of your control," I explained, leaning back on the rail of the ramp.

"What's happened?" he asked, straightening up and pointing toward the interior of the building. "We only have about a weeks' worth of work left. Our target date is fine on my end."

I held up my hand. "I know and I want you to go ahead and finish the job. I'm sure you have other jobs to move on to. I'm waiting on the sign for the roof," I explained lamely.

He slid his hammer into his belt loop and eyed me. "Well, now I think you can probably open without that sign, boy. Everyone in the town is expecting ya to open soon."

I crossed my ankles and nodded. "I'll be opening soon. I just need a little more time. I need to get the employees trained, and the time I've spent with Savannah has put me back a little. I'm calling in a friend to help me get the back of the house trained in, and I've hired a front of the house manager, too. I don't want to rush them, though. The grand opening has to go off without a hitch."

Big Eddie flipped the top open on his water bottle and took a swig. "How is Mrs. Kiss doing? We were all really worried about her, but April kept us informed. Ms. Hart, err, Kiss, has a real good heart, and we hope she's feeling better."

"She was very touched when she got the bouquet of flowers from you and the crew at the hospital. Savannah is having a hard time dealing with the aftermath of what happened, so I'm trying to spend as much time as I can with her until she feels better."

Big Eddie leaned up against the doorjamb and stared out over the parking lot. "That ex of hers really messed her up. I may go to hell for saying it, but I'm glad he's dead. He got what he deserved when that log took him out. Maybe he got off too easy if you ask me. My wife's first husband was like that, he didn't die in a nice way, either. I don't think karma likes it when you go about hitting women."

I stood up a little straighter. "Your wife was in an abusive relationship?"

He rubbed his hand on his jeans. "She sure was.

I met her at the grocery store when I was working one day. She was carrying a little one on her hip and sporting a torn lip and bruised face. I followed her out to her car and told her she didn't have to stay with him. I think she thought I was crazy, cause twenty years ago, nobody talked about it. I guess she wasn't too put off considering she married me."

I shook my finger at him. "Is your wife around town, Eddie?"

"Yeah, yeah, she works at the bank now. Head teller," he said proudly, and I clapped him on the shoulder.

"If I bring Savannah to the emporium tomorrow, do you think your wife, what's her name?" I stopped and asked.

"Virginia. We call her Gina."

"Do you think Gina would come over and talk to Savannah? Has she ever done that before, counseled other women?" I asked, an idea forming.

"She does it all the time for the women's shelter in Rochester. She's always running here and there. She mentioned to me when I told her that Mrs. Kiss had surgery, she should stop in and talk with her."

A smile tugged at my lips. "You have my cell number. Have her call me tonight? I'll give her a little history, and set up a time to have Savannah there when it's convenient for Gina. Maybe Savannah just needs to talk to someone who has lived through it and came out the other side as strong as Gina has."

He nodded in agreement. "My Gina is a strong one, but I'll tell you a secret, Ms. Savannah is stronger. The things she still endures because of him, well, that ain't right. She's been really down the last few months, then you came along and she started smiling again. Gina will do whatever she can to make sure she keeps smiling."

"That's what I needed to hear, Eddie. Savannah's self-esteem has taken a hard hit finding out that her face will never be normal again. She's pushing me away and hard as I try, I can't get her to understand that I love her regardless." I punched the handrail with my fist and leaned on my palms, breathing deep.

"Well, I'll be damned," Big Eddie whistled. "You are in love with her."

I closed my eyes and took a steadying breath, "Of course, I'm in love with her. I married her, didn't I?"

Eddie leaned against the rail next to me. "There are a lot of reasons why a man might marry a woman. There was some talk around the watercooler that your reasons might not have been love. I told them they were wrong, and you just proved it."

"I don't much care what people were saying around the watercooler, Eddie. They can think whatever they want, but I will not lose that woman to the ghost of a man who never deserved to have her to start with," I growled.

He slapped me on the back and squeezed my

shoulder. "You can count on Gina to make sure that doesn't happen. If I can give you one piece of advice?" he asked, and I half-nodded, half-shrugged. "Don't stop telling her how you feel. This is all new to her. Being loved for who she is, I mean. A battered woman's self-esteem doesn't even exist after being in a situation like that. It took Gina a good long time before she stopped cringing when I came at her too fast, or to believe me when I told her she was beautiful and smart. It's not easy sometimes, but you were picked for her for a reason. Try to keep that in mind when you're frustrated because twenty years later, I can tell you, it's all worth it."

I stood up straight and stuck my hand out to him. "Thank you, Eddie. I guess it's true what they say, often the person we least expect to understand is the one who understands the most."

Eddie shook my hand firmly then gave me a firm pat on the back. "I know you're a big city boy, but around here, we take care of each other. We'll get Ms. Savannah smiling again, together."

"I hope you're right, Eddie. I hope you're right," I muttered, shoving my hands in my pockets and trudging down the ramp.

Savannah

I walked through the door of my shop and

the smell of fresh roses filled the small space. The coolers were filled with bouquets ready for the holiday. I took a moment and did a full three-sixty, hardly believing what I was seeing. "Thank you so much for everything you've done, April," I said when I turned back to the counter.

"It was my pleasure, Savannah. I've had a lot of fun over the last few weeks letting my creative side through."

"I'm glad you enjoyed your time here. I know you singlehandedly saved my business for me. Did you get the flower delivery already for Saturday?" I asked and she nodded, pointing to the coolers.

"It came in earlier, so I put all the special-order flowers in the back cooler and everything else in their respective places. I made the same amount of premade bouquets as you sold last year, figuring you could add to that as you see fit. I hope it helps." She picked up her purse and I went around the counter, hugging her tightly.

"You don't know how much it helps." I pulled back to tell her, so she could see my lips.

"Are you sure you're going to be okay here this afternoon? Noel said you aren't supposed to be working yet." April fidgeted with her purse and I patted her shoulder.

"Dr. Kent said I can work part-time as long as I'm careful, so yes, I'll be just fine. I will close tonight and come in tomorrow for a few hours to help make the special orders I don't get done today. You should take Saturday off, Noel and I will work

Valentine's Day," I assured her and she shrugged.

"I don't mind working if you need help. I can make deliveries or whatever you need. I don't have any plans." She stared down at the floor and I put my arm around her.

"I would love your help with deliveries. We can make a shorter day of it if you want to do that for me." I walked her to the door.

"I want to help so you and Noel can celebrate Valentine's Day together. It will also be your one-month anniversary," she said excitedly.

"You're right," I tried to smile, but just couldn't do it, "and we both appreciate how much you've done to help us this last month. I'll see you tomorrow?"

"I'll be here at ten to open, and I'll see you whenever you get here." April waved and disappeared down the sidewalk toward Noel's café.

"Right, so here I am," I said aloud to the empty room.

I walked behind the counter and clicked the computer on, waiting for the pleasant feeling to come over me that I usually get being with my flowers. I read through the orders and sent the specialty jobs to the printer and waited. Still nothing.

I pulled one of my aprons down off the hook and tied it around my waist, walking to the cooler and picking a white gardenia from the bucket. The mirror that hung on the wall, reflecting the many hanging baskets, was in front of me and for the first time, I forced myself to look.

I stepped closer to the mirror and stared at myself for a moment before dropping my eyes. I cleared my throat, and clipped the stem off the gardenia then fastened it in my hair, just like I used to do every day. For the first time, instead of it holding back one side of my long hair, it sat closer to my ear, holding back the small swath of hair Crow had left.

I dropped my hands, hating how I felt ugly in such a beautiful place. Mostly, I hated that I felt ugly and didn't know how to change that. I gathered up some flowers for the first special-order, taking them back to the counter and laying them out in order, going back for the baby's breath and greens. Snipping stems and arranging the flowers felt good after too many weeks away from my work, and I let my mind wander to when I first opened this emporium.

I was barely out of business school and working two jobs to save money. When this building opened up, I got a business loan for women and opened Savannah's Flower Emporium on nothing more than a wing and a prayer.

The first year was rocky not being able to afford any employees, but soon the community was supporting me enough to be able to hire some part-time help. On my first day off in almost a year, I went to the library and checked out books about how to improve your business, then went with Snow to dinner in Rochester. That's where I met Günther, the man I fell completely and madly in love with over the next six months, or so I thought.

In the moments when I was honest with myself, I knew he was controlling and short-tempered, but in the moments when he showered me with affection, I convinced myself he was the one for me.

When he proposed a year later with a giant diamond ring, I couldn't get the ring on fast enough, keeping the questioning thoughts at bay. Snow tried to tiptoe around the way he treated me without straight out discouraging me, but I ignored it all.

It was two weeks after the wedding when he hit me the first time. I shrugged it off when he apologized with flowers and wine, but over the next year, the episodes escalated to the point I spent a lot of time learning makeup techniques to cover the bruises.

I pulled down a heart covered vase from the shelf and filled the bottom with red and clear rocks, carrying it to the sink to fill with water.

Hearts.

My maiden name was Hart, and after the divorce was official, I changed my name back. I wanted to forget about that time in my life, not the lessons I learned, just the pain I endured. In the end, changing my name didn't repair the damage he had done, not by a long shot. Now my last name was Kiss, and I didn't know what to do about it.

Noel has spent the last two weeks since the surgery taking care of me all day, and holding me all night. I've been trying to push him away and pull him to me at the same time, and that isn't fair. He's the most wonderful man I've ever known and for whatever reason, he still believes that our journey will have a happy ending.

I want to believe it at night when he's holding me and telling me he loves me and wants to take care of me, but when the sun comes up, I know he can see who I really am. There's a possibility he will decide he doesn't want to be saddled with a damaged woman who has little to offer him. He's so much smarter than I am, and I feel inferior all of the time. He says that's my problem because that's not how he feels at all. I guess the whole thing is my problem. I just don't know what to do about it.

I heard pounding next door and stared out the window for a moment, forgetting that Big Eddie and his crew were finishing the café. Noel pushed back the grand opening a few weeks because of me. He tried to tell me he needed more time to get the staff trained and the paperwork in order. I might not be as smart as he is, but I could see that for what it was. He'd spent so much of the last month with me that his business suffered because of it.

I sighed and finished the first order, carrying it to the cooler in the back and setting it in the special-order bin. One down, ninety-eight more to go, I thought, heading back out to the front. I was just thankful my incision wasn't bothering me today and I was able to cut back on the medication that made me so tired. I stopped short at the counter when I noticed I wasn't alone.

"Hi, Gina." I waved at the older lady standing near the rose cooler. "Looking for anything special today?" I asked, walking toward her.

She turned with her hand on the cooler door, her face lit up in a smile. "Savannah, so good to see you," she cooed, pulling me into a hug.

Gina was the head teller at Snowberry Bank and Loan, and the wife of the guy making all the racket next door. I motioned toward the café.

"Your husband seems to be bringing down the house today." I grinned and she laughed, her perfectly coiffed hair bouncing in rhythm.

"He's determined to finish that job. He says he still has two days to win those free pancakes." She laughed, slapping her leg.

"I have it on good authority Noel gave him all the time he needs to finish and upheld his promise for free pancakes. I think he's in competition with himself," I joked, and she held out her palms.

"You would think right. He mostly just wants to get the café done as quickly as he can for Noel. He knows he needs to get it open soon." She leaned against the counter and inspected all the flowers I had set out.

"That's super sweet of him but it's not him holding up the show, it's me. I've been taking up all of Noel's time and he hasn't been able to devote the time to the café that it needs," I explained, snipping stems with more precision than was necessary.

"Eddie is very sweet. Most people don't know it, though. They always judge him by his size and gruffness before they really get to know him." She picked up a flower and inhaled deeply. "He saved me from a life of hell, you know."

I glanced up quickly, my snippers stopping mid-snip. "No, I don't know. What do you mean?"

She leaned over the counter and handed me the flower. "When I met Eddie, I was a young mother who was struggling to get out of a bad marriage."

I laid the flower and clippers down, wiping my hands on my apron. "Really? I had no idea. You mean Eddie isn't Landon's real father?"

She shook her head. "No, Eddie adopted Landon when he was about four, so that's why he has the same last name, but he's not his biological father. Not that it matters much, in my opinion."

It was my turn to shake my head. "No, I was just surprised, that's all. There's always a big difference between being able to father a child and actually parenting the child."

"You got that right. You have experience?" she asked, pulling up a stool and perching her ample bottom on it.

"My dad was a real piece of work, so yeah, I have firsthand experience. He never should have gotten married or had a kid. He couldn't see past his own wants," I explained, pulling up a stool myself. I still got tired quickly if I overdid it.

"How are you doing, Savannah? You look a little more comfortable than the last time I saw you." She smiled, patting my hand.

I put my hand up to my face and covered my cheek a little. "I'm feeling better. Thank you for asking."

She pointed at my hand, her finger waving in a circle. "Does it hurt you? Should I call Noel?"

I let my hand fall to my lap and busied myself with a flower. "We don't need to bother Noel. It doesn't hurt. I'm just self-conscious, I guess."

"Self-conscious about what?" she asked, looking closer at my face.

I picked up a new flower and didn't make eye contact. "You have to notice how my face just hangs there."

She shrugged slightly and leaned back. "When you smile, I notice the right side doesn't go up, but you know what? I would much rather see it that way than the way it was the last time I saw you. You had to have been in so much pain, it just broke my heart."

I glanced from the flower to her. "I was in a lot of pain, but that's gone now. Dr. Kent had to sever this nerve to save my eye." I motioned at the spot and she nodded.

"He did an excellent job. He's one of the best. I've worked with him a lot over the years," she remarked and picked up another flower.

"What? Why? Did you have a problem, too?" I asked, surprised.

"Honey, my husband beat me daily, sometimes

several times a day, but I wasn't a patient of Dr. Kent's. I work with several of the women's shelters in the area and he's our expert when we need him for court. He is also our go-to doctor when there's facial trauma."

I sat dumbfounded and stared at her. "I had no idea you did that. How did I not know this?"

She chuckled. "I've done it for so long I don't think anyone even thinks about it anymore. The closest shelter is in Rochester anyway, so I'm there a lot."

I thought back to the last time we were there to see Dr. Kent. "I met a woman in the waiting room a few days ago. She was getting ready to have cosmetic surgery on her face. Her ex-husband had thrown acid in her face, blinding and scarring her."

"That was one of the worst acts of domestic abuse I've ever had to be part of. Her name is Ruth and that was about seven years ago now. She's really an amazing testament of the human spirit."

"She was so upbeat and happy. Her husband was with her and struck up a conversation with Noel. I was a little bit surprised to see her married again after all of that," I admitted.

"I'm married again. Very happily for the last twenty years. When Eddie met me, I was one giant bruise. That day in the grocery store, I was trying to find a ride to Rochester to the women's shelter. The night before, my ex got mad about the baby crying. If I hadn't protected Landon, he would probably be dead. I couldn't risk my child any longer and decided I needed to get away."

I leaned closer and propped my arms on the counter. "Did you find a ride?"

She made the so-so sign. "No one was heading to Rochester, so I was walking back to our car. I couldn't risk taking the car all the way to Rochester. He would find me and know where the shelter was. I was out of ideas when Eddie walked up to my car. He said *you don't have to stay with him. I'll help you.*"

"What did you do?" I asked, entranced by the story.

"He followed me to the house with his truck. When we got there, my husband was at work and Eddie held Landon while I quickly packed a bag for each of us. I left the keys for the car on the counter and Eddie drove us to the shelter. I stayed there for a month while I healed, and they helped me through the trials of getting a divorce from a man who didn't want to admit he was at fault. When it was time to leave the shelter, Eddie was there to pick me up. He took me to his little apartment and gave Landon and me his bedroom while he slept on the couch. What I would have done without him, I don't know, but I'm glad he was there that day." She smiled and I nodded.

"I'm glad it worked out for you, it isn't always that easy," I mumbled, getting another vase down and filling it with pebbles.

"You made it look pretty easy. Your wedding was beautiful and Noel is so much in love with you," she pointed out, but I didn't take my eyes off my work.

"It's anything but easy, Gina. I won't be married to Noel much longer." It physically hurt to say it, and I forced the words through my teeth.

Her hands came toward my face and I jumped back, knocking over two vases in the process and landing on my elbow.

"Savannah!" Gina cried, coming around to where I laid on the floor. "I'm sorry, my goodness. Oh, let me help," she fussed and I waved her away and stood up, being careful of the broken glass.

"It's okay, Gina. I'm fine," I assured her, brushing off my hands and grabbing the broom, sweeping the glass into a pile and leaving it there until later.

"Does Noel hit you?" she asked quietly. "Is that why you're leaving him?"

My hands started to shake and I grasped them together. "No, he's nothing like Günther. He would never hurt me. You have to believe me. He's been nothing but kind, supportive, and loving. I just overreacted when I saw your hand coming at me. I get dizzy easily," I explained lamely.

She took hold of my shaking hand and led me back to the stool. "If he's kind, supportive, and loving, why are you leaving him then? Don't you love him?" she asked perplexed.

I sat down hard on the stool, all of my energy gone after the adrenaline rush from the fall. "I love him more than I've ever loved anyone else in my life, Gina."

She squatted down so she could look me in the eye. "Then why? Does he know you want out?"

My chin trembled and I worked to hold it steady. "I can't ask him to stay with me. He married me thinking that after the surgery, my face would be normal and the evidence of the last man would be gone. He married me thinking we could live our life without daily reminders of the biggest mistake of my life. But now," I motioned at my face, "now I'll always look like this. Every time he looks at me, he will see the damage of another man. I'm beyond repair, Gina. I can't ask him to deal with this every day for the rest of his life."

"Deal with what?" she asked sadly.

"My face!" I pushed on my face, angrily. "This is my punishment, not his. He deserves more." I broke down in tears and she hugged me to her chest, rubbing my back.

"Savannah, sweetheart, you're breaking my heart. You're not being punished. Don't you see? Günther was the work of the devil. The devil had control of that man and his soul, not yours. Noel's arms will offer you solace. Does Noel make you feel safe?" she asked softly.

"I didn't know what safe felt like until the first time he put his arms around me. I was in terrible pain, but they comforted me," I shared honestly.

"Do you understand you deserve to be happy?" she asked and I nodded slowly.

"Everyone keeps telling me that." I hiccupped

and wiped my eyes.

"What keeps you from believing them?"

"My whole life has been filled with people who were nice to me because they felt sorry for me," I explained. "So much, so I guess I can't tell the difference anymore."

"Do you think Dully married Snow because he feels sorry for her?" Gina asked, and I gasped.

"Why would you say that? Of course not! Dully would give his life for Snow. Do you see the way he looks at her?" I struggled to stand, trying to defend my friend.

She held me down with her hands on my shoulders. "I asked because you know that look in Dully's eyes?" She waited until I nodded and then went on, "That's the same look I see in Noel's eyes when he gazes at you. He didn't marry you out of pity. He married you out of love." She ran her hand down my face and I tried not to flinch. "This isn't stopping him from loving you. Why are you letting it stop you from loving him?"

"Because she's scared," Noel said from the doorway. I whipped around, surprised by the intrusion. "If I was her, I'd be scared, too. She's gone through hell and still is, but I'm not going anywhere."

He came around the counter and put his arms around me. "Noel, what are you doing here?" I whispered against his belly.

"I'm always going to be here, I told you that. There will never be a time when you need me that

I won't be here. If I show you that enough times maybe, someday, you'll believe me."

Gina rubbed my back and spoke to Noel. "I'm not sure she's ready to be back to work."

"I'm going to take her home. April is on her way in. She's had enough for today," he told her and I tried to interject.

"I need to stay. I have to get these flowers done," I sighed, wiping my eyes and straightening my shoulders. "This is one of my busiest times of the year. I have to fill these orders."

"April will work on them the rest of the afternoon while you rest. If we do it in spells, it will keep you from getting so tired," Noel said firmly, and I could see there would be no arguing.

Gina rubbed my shoulder and knelt down in front of me. "I'm glad I stopped in today and that we got to talk, but I'm sorry you got so tired. Promise me you'll think about what we talked about? If you ever need to talk, call me, day or night. I'm always here for you."

I hugged her shoulders carefully. "Thank you, Gina, for everything you do for us. It's not a club I wanted to be part of, but now that I am, at least I know there are wonderful women like you who care about me."

"I do care about you, and I want you to be happy, just like I am, and like so many other women in this club," which she put in quotation marks. "In the meantime, rest and let Noel take care of you. The people of Snowberry are behind you one hundred percent." She stood and patted Noel on the shoulder before heading to the door.

"Gina, did you need flowers? You must have come in for a reason," I called to her, and she stopped with her hand on the door handle.

"I came in because I knew you were hurting. I didn't know why, but I knew I needed to see you. You helped me today, Savannah. Thank you for reminding me that I have a lot of work left to do in this club. I want you to remember that Noel's arms are a sanctuary for your heart, and you deserve all the happiness he has to offer you."

Chapter Sixteen

Noel

"Seems like you've been up to lots of behind the scene things," Savannah said from the couch where she was looking at the mail.

By the time I got her home, she was nearly asleep in the seat next to me. I put her to bed for a nap, then checked in with Dr. Kent's nurse. She had assured me it was typical of this type of surgery to get worn out quickly, which is why they recommend six weeks off work afterward. Today was barely two weeks, but convincing Savannah she needed more time off wasn't working. I had to take matters into my own hands.

"I don't know what you mean." I sat next to her and picked up a catalog for elegant vases.

"Is that so?" she asked, turning and giving me the once over. "You know nothing about April showing up with Claire, my previous employee?"

"April mentioned that maybe we might need more help for Valentine's Day. I told her if she knew someone she could trust, to let me know. I had no idea Claire was an old employee. Did you fire her, or did she move onto something else?"

She leaned her head back against the couch. "She was the employee I had to let go when I got into trouble with the mortgage. I decided if I didn't pay an employee, I could swing it, but even that wasn't enough."

I rubbed her thigh slowly and patiently. "I didn't know that, but I'm glad she was willing to come back and help. I talked to Dr. Kent's nurse and she said you might be pushing it too fast. I know you have to be there for Saturday, so if the girls can get the majority of the orders done, that will be helpful. We can both work Saturday, and you can rest in the back when you get worn out. We'll get through it," I promised.

She nodded and leaned forward, laying her lips on mine. Her eyes went closed and she wound her hand behind my head. For the first time, she kissed me. I pulled her onto my lap and cradled her back in my arms, enjoying the softness of her body against mine and the sweet taste of her lips. She leaned back and gazed into my eyes for quite possibly the first time. We sat there like that for a long time, her eyes locked with mine and my hand tracing the angles of her face.

"What do you see?" I asked her softly, bringing her hand to my lips for a kiss.

"Gina told me she can see how much you love me in your eyes. She said it's the same way Dully looks at Snow. I thought maybe if I looked long enough and hard enough, I would learn how to tell the difference."

"Tell what difference?" I asked, surprised.

"The difference between love and pity. I've lived my whole life with people being nice to me because they pity me. I don't know how to tell the difference anymore."

"Did it work?"

"Did what work?"

"Looking in my eyes."

"You have very truthful eyes." She glanced down at her hands in mine and back to my eyes. "Did you know Gina was married before Eddie?"

I nodded. "He told me that yesterday. Not knowing them for very long probably meant I was less surprised than you were."

She laughed a little. "True, I've known them forever, and their son Landon. I had no idea Eddie wasn't his real father. Turns out, Gina is a battered woman, too. I say is because I think a little part of us always remains that way even years later. It changes our self-esteem and it takes a long time to get that back, if we ever do."

"I get that, which is why I know it will take time for you to believe the things I'm saying are true, but they are. I love you and I know you're meant for me." I kissed her lips slowly until she relented and let me take full control. I kept the kiss hot, our tongues fighting each other until I had to break us apart. She was panting heavily and rubbing herself against me. "You didn't answer my question," I said, taking her chin, so she had to make eye contact. "Did my eyes show you the difference between pity and love?" I asked point-blank.

She laid her hand against my chest, her hand warm through the thin fabric of my t-shirt. "Your eyes tell me what your heart has shown me."

I leaned down and kissed her tenderly. "That coming to Snowberry wasn't just a whim? Maybe I came to Snowberry because our hearts, our souls, were connected the moment we met and longed to be together? Making your heart feel happy, safe, and secure is the only thing that matters to me. If I have to give up my business to do it, I will. That being this much in love with someone this quickly is scary, wonderful, earth-shattering, mind-blowing, and worth the risk? That I take my job as your husband, your protector, and your sanctuary, very seriously and will never let anyone hurt you ever again?"

She reached up and held her hand to my face. "I wished for that all to be true," she whispered, "I want nothing more than for it to be true. I want to experience your love without feeling scared."

I gathered her close to me and held her in my arms, my lips against her ear. "How do you feel now?"

"I feel like I never want to leave this space. Like everything outside the door doesn't matter, and I can close my eyes and not be afraid."

"Have you ever felt this way before?" I asked, kissing her neck, and her pulse thrummed against my lips.

"The first time I felt this way was when you held me all night long and never let go. It's why I can't sleep at night without you holding me. Your arms take away my pain so I can sleep."

"That's because we were made for each other. The way we met and married may have been fast, but the connection our souls have is anything but. If you hadn't gone through the things you did with Günther, you might not have recognized the feeling of safety when I held you. If I hadn't gone through a relationship with no connection, I might not have recognized the spark in my heart as real, true love. If I hadn't made amends with December, I wouldn't have been here for you. I had to fix the situation with December in order to meet you. What if I hadn't done that? That's what scares me the most and why I jumped in with both feet. My destination my whole life, was you. The road wasn't straight, it had many hills and valleys I had to walk through, but your heart, soul, and body were my reward."

I turned her into me, so I could kiss her, my body fighting to be one with hers when our tongues touched. I moaned and she pressed herself closer to me, her lips like butter under mine, melted and sweet. I was about to carry her to the bedroom when the doorbell rang.

She pulled away, her breathing heavy, and her face flushed. "We should get that."

I let out a deep breath. "I can't get up right now without embarrassing myself," I admitted.

She smiled the most beautiful smile. It was a smile of pleasure and happiness that she was the one who had done these things to me.

I watched her walk to the door and pull it open, but it didn't help the condition I was currently in. The sway of her body, the way she moved so fluidly, left me wondering how she would feel under me, around me. She spoke to whoever was at the door and her voice was like honey. I knew the sound of her calling my name when we finally joined together would be sweeter than anything I'd ever heard before.

"Noel? Noel?" I glanced up and almost ran to the door, wondering how many times she had called me.

"Bram is here." She motioned at the man who stood inside the door with a big box.

I cleared my throat. "Hi, Bram. How's it going?" I asked my cheeks bright red.

He was grinning like he already knew our secret. "I'm just fine. Sorry to interrupt your day, but I meant to bring this over sooner." He leaned the box up against the couch and handed Savannah an envelope.

"What's this?" she asked, and he crossed his arms across his chest.

"It's a wedding gift from the Alexanders. You'll understand why it took this long to get it when you see it. We've considered you part of the family for the last four years, Savannah, and we couldn't be happier that our sister is finally with the person she was meant to be with."

Savannah hugged Bram tightly and looked at me with more curiosity than fear in her eyes. "Thank you, Bram. You didn't have to do that, but I'm sure we'll love it."

He pulled back and motioned to it when his phone went off. He checked the message and sighed. "Looks like you'll have to discover what's inside without me. I have to head back to the press."

Savannah walked with him to the door. "Everything all right?" she asked as he turned the knob and stepped onto the stoop.

"Breaking story, not sure what about yet, but that's the nature of the business. Have a great afternoon."

She handed me the envelope. "Maybe you should open it. I know the Alexanders and I might cry," she joked, but I could tell she was serious, so I opened it and pulled out the letter.

"Dear Savannah and Noel, inside this package is the beginning of your life together. The moment you first saw each other, the moment of your first kiss, and the moment when you became one are what we see, but what we feel is trust and knowledge that love will conquer all. When times are tough or when you need a reminder about love everlasting, we hope these memories of your beginning will carry you through forever. With all our love and best wishes, the Alexanders."

She glanced up at me with tears in her eyes and

gave me the palms up. "Told you, they get me every time."

I chuckled a little and kissed the tears off her face, then pulled out my pocketknife and sliced through the tape. She watched me from the other side of the box and then pulled back the flap and peered in.

"Oh..." She sighed and I reached in and pulled out a photo album, handing it to her.

She sat down on the couch with it on her lap and ran her hand over the front of it. It was inscribed with our names and the date of the wedding in gold script, a picture of us in the corner. Before she could open it, I carefully sliced through the bubble wrap on a large frame, kicked the box aside and sat down by her. The frame matched the book and the picture was the same, but it was breathtaking in a poster size format.

She barely squeaked when she saw it, her hand going to her mouth and her eyes filling with tears. It was the picture from our wedding night on the bridge when the moonbeam had lain across our shoulders and our eyes were locked together. The caption at the bottom read, "Forever bound by love. Two hearts and two souls are now one."

I pulled the sticky note off it and read it aloud. "I entered this in a photo contest recently. I'm just a small-town photographer for a newspaper, but this picture needs to be seen by the world. It's the very essence of love. B."

"Wow." She breathed out, wiping the tears

from her face.

"You're so beautiful. I could stare at you all day and never tire of your beauty," I admitted.

"It's such an amazing photo."

"Savannah, I'm not looking at the photo," I whispered and she glanced away from it long enough to see me watching her. "I'm looking at you looking at the photo, and I've never seen you so unlocked to your emotions. You see your beauty in this photo, don't you?"

She nodded, her hand hovering over her face. I reached over and lowered her hand to her lap. "Don't hide, Savannah. My God, you're so loved. You have to see it, don't you? You have to see how many people in this town see your beauty, and rely on your beauty. Not just your physical beauty, either. They rely on the beauty in your heart because it's what they need to see in the windows of the town, gracing the tables of the anniversary couples, the bedsides of the sick, and comforting the grieving. If you don't feel that beauty in here," I tapped her chest, "none of us can experience it out here."

I rested the picture against the coffee table and she stood quickly, nearly tipping backward. I caught her and steadied her. When she had her bearings, she gazed at me, a new resolve in her eyes. "I'll be right back," she assured me, but I held her arm.

"Where are you going?"

She pointed to the garage. "To get a hammer

and nails, so we can hang the picture."

She smiled widely and I took hold of both of her arms and held her there.

"You're going to hang the picture? You don't put pictures up in your house," I pointed out, completely shocked.

She pointed to the fireplace where the mantle sat nearly void of any photos. "I put photos up in my house. I have photos of Snow, Dully, and Sunny, but I only put up photos of people I love," she explained happily.

I could hear in her voice that she believed the words she was saying.

"You're going to hang it and I'll watch. I think we should put it above the fireplace. What do you think?"

"I think it's the perfect place, and I know I couldn't love you more than I do right now."

"Now, that was a crazy day." I grinned, squeezing her hand.

"Crazy? It was downright mad." She giggled and then sighed. "Not that I'm complaining. I probably made three months' worth of income in one day. Did you see the coolers when we left?"

"It looked like a tornado had gone through the place. All I saw were a few petals and even fewer leaves. Are you even going to open tomorrow?"

I asked, pulling the truck into the driveway and shutting off the engine.

"Not much sense. The day after Valentine's Day is always a zero sales day. Since I don't have any flowers left, I have to wait until Monday for a shipment. I will probably go in and try to get things cleaned and straightened up, though."

I turned in the seat and took her hand. "How about if you let me and April go in and clean and straighten things, so you can rest. Today must have worn you right out."

She leaned in and kissed me. "I'm tired, yes, but it's a good tired. I haven't felt good tired like I've really worked hard for a long time. I'll sleep good tonight, but I'm not in pain."

I caressed her cheek, enjoying her new openness to my touch. Since we hung the photo from Bram on the wall, it was like it had flipped a switch inside her. She smiled now, all the time, and she spent hours going through the photo album with Snow yesterday, even going as far as making an order of pictures to be delivered. It was a start and one I planned on taking advantage of tonight.

"I was going to take you out to dinner tonight, but I knew you'd be tired. Maybe I can have a rain check?" I asked.

She rolled her head toward me. "You knew right, and I'd love a rain check. Maybe we can take a trip down to Rochester next weekend before the grand opening? A little getaway for a night before the craziness of a new café opening."

"I would love that. Come on, let's go inside, it's getting cold out here." I motioned her out of the truck and walked her up the path, her arm through mine. The door was open and the light from the fireplace glowed through the screen door. She stopped suddenly and pointed at the door.

"Someone's been here. I locked the door this morning." Her voice was shaky and I kissed her temple.

"Someone has been here, but not the way you're thinking. Come inside."

She gave me a hand on hip, but finally stepped up on the first step and waited for me to get the door. I pulled it open and ushered her inside, where she stopped just a few steps in the door. She surveyed the room and turned to me, her mouth agape.

"What's all of this?" she asked stupefied.

"Happy Valentine's Day, sweetheart. It's our first, and I wanted to make it memorable." I pulled her coat off her shoulders, hanging it up.

She wandered into the room and smelled the gardenias on the kitchen table. She noticed the photos lined up on the island, all framed like she and Snow had planned out yesterday. She picked up a picture of the two of us dancing our first dance on our wedding night and hugged it to her.

"I can't believe you did all of this for me." She turned and I saw the tears in her eyes.

"I didn't do it all. I had some help," I teased.

"Snow." She grinned and I nodded.

"Snow, December, and Susie had a ball today, I'm pretty sure." I took the frame from her hand and set it back down. "I think Snow was so excited that you wanted pictures she didn't want to give you a chance to change your mind."

I pulled her into me and she planted her hands on my chest. "I smell." She wrinkled her nose and I kissed it.

"I didn't notice," I teased and she blushed.

"Do I have time for a shower before we eat?"

"We have all night. Go ahead. I'll pour the wine when I hear you shut off the water." I patted her butt as she walked toward the hallway and she turned, her eyes roving over me with a smile on her face.

When I heard the water go on, I pulled out my phone and texted Snow, thanking her for taking time out of the day to make Savannah so happy. I closed the front door and turned some music on, getting out the fruit and cheese from the fridge and bringing it to the coffee table with glasses and plates.

My phone vibrated and I checked the messages. All she sent were kissy lips, hearts, and a kissing couple emoji. I laughed, but got the message. I sat down on the couch and stared at the picture of us again. Every time I saw it, she took my breath away. I wasn't sure of much, but I was sure of one thing, I wanted to be the last man she married. I heard the water turn off and I got the wine, pulling the cork from the bottle and bringing it back to the table. I heard her soft footsteps and then she found me in the living room. I set the bottle down hard on the table when I saw her.

I took a step back and tried to look away, but I couldn't, my eyes were glued to her. "You don't like it," she stated, backing up to the hallway and I reached my hand out.

"I love it. In fact, I love it so much I'm at a loss for words," I whispered.

She stood before me in a long white silk robe. Roses were cascading down the front, just like her wedding dress, but it was the promise of what was underneath that left me breathless.

"It's stunning. When did you pick it up?" I asked, motioning her toward me. When she got close enough, I pulled her in to dance with me.

"You didn't buy it for me?" she asked, laying her head on my shoulder.

I laughed softly and kissed her temple. "No, I wish I could take credit for it, but I can't. My gosh, I can hardly breathe with you in my arms right now."

She pulled back and gazed at me. "If you didn't buy it, then who left it in the bathroom..."

We both started to snicker and I wrapped my arms all the way around her and whispered *Snow* in her ear.

"That girl always has something up her sleeve."

"Remind me to thank her," I groaned, running my hands down her back, the silky material gliding under my hands. I knew she wasn't wearing a bra or panties and I closed my eyes, trying to rein in my desire.

"I think we should have some wine," she said after she cleared her throat. She stepped away from me and poured two glasses then sat down on the couch. I joined her and we sipped the wine, ate cheese and fruit, and talked about all the fun couples we met today.

"I think my favorite couple was the mystery couple." She set her plate and glass down on the coffee table.

"The mystery couple?" I asked coyly.

"Yeah, you know three pink roses, no thorns, tubes, no vase, and a yellow ribbon. I'm bummed I didn't get to see who picked it up. Orders like that always make me wonder what the story is behind it."

She was relaxed from the wine, her eyes closed, and a lazy smile on her face as she pictured in her mind who might have ordered that bouquet.

I opened the door of the coffee table and reached in, pulling out my first surprise. "Maybe I can tell you the story?"

Her eyes fluttered open and her mouth fell a few inches when she saw me holding three pink roses, no thorns, with a yellow ribbon. She sat up and I held the flowers out to her.

"There's this woman, this most amazing woman, who has come into my life and stolen my heart. This is our first Valentine's together and I wanted to make sure she knew how much I loved her. I got three pink roses, the first to symbolize first love because I truly believe you are my first love. The second rose symbolizes innocence. I know you think you have no innocence left, but you're wrong. I see your innocence every time I watch your eyes fall closed when you relax into my arms. The third and final rose, and the most important, symbolizes healing. Healing of your body, but hopefully also your heart and soul. There are no thorns because I would never do anything to hurt you. The yellow ribbon is purely for me because it reminds me that I am your protector and you are my joy."

She brought the flowers to her nose and closed her eyes. "That's an even better story than I ever imagined."

I stayed on the floor and pulled a box from under the table as well, clearing my throat. "I'm glad you liked that story. I have something else to give you, but you have to open your eyes."

She opened them slowly and took in the sight before her. Her eyes darted between my hand holding the box and my face several times, but she said nothing.

"Savannah, the first time I proposed, I didn't do it the way you deserved for it to be done. You deserve romance, wine, flowers, and diamonds, but even those things cannot outshine your beauty. You have the most amazing sparkle. Even when you're tired and worn out, it's still there, making the world a brighter place. Your empathy towards others, even when you're worse off than they are, is the most beautiful part of you in my eyes. I have no doubt our children are going to be so lucky to be in your arms, to have you as their mommy, because you will strive every day to protect them, love them, and teach them about life. You will show them how to be shining examples of love in the world, consider everyone an equal, and never waste an opportunity. You've taught me that in just the short time I've known you. Tonight, I'm not wasting the opportunity to tell you I want to be the man who protects you, loves you and helps you teach our children about life. Savannah, I love you with a power I didn't know I had inside me on December twenty-third, but all that changed on Christmas Eve. Will you honor me for the rest of my life and be my wife?"

Tears ran down her face as she laid the flowers on the couch and crawled onto the floor in front of me. She took my face in her hands and gazed into my eyes for so long I worried she was thinking of a way to say no. Finally, she smiled through her tears and nodded.

"I would love nothing more than to be your wife for the rest of my life," she cried happily.

I let out a sigh of relief and she sat back, staring at the ring I still held in front of me. I pulled it from the box and held it up so she could see it. "It matches this one, doesn't it?" she asked, holding up her hand where her wedding band was.

"It's the ring that was supposed to come first.

Remember, Kay told us that's the anniversary band?" She nodded and smiled a little at the memory. "We might have done things backward, but tonight I want to do them right."

She held out her hand for me to put it on, and I took it, kissing her hand. I touched the band on her finger. "This ring was blessed when we said our vows in front of everyone we know." I held up the new ring. "This ring hasn't been blessed, so tonight I want to do that, just you and me. I want to say the words that will wed us spiritually, not just legally." I cleared my throat and held her hand to my chest. "I, Noel Christopher Kiss, take you, Savannah, to be my wife. To have and to hold from this day forward, to love and to protect, to smile and to laugh, in sickness and in health, in good times and in bad. I give you my heart, my soul, and my promise to love you always, keep you safe, and give you the life you deserve by offering you unconditional love for a lifetime. With this ring, I thee wed." I slipped the ring on her finger, where it nestled perfectly with the band.

She was crying so many tears I pulled a tissue out of the box on the floor and she wiped her eyes, laughing a little while she did it. Then she picked up my hand, working the band off my finger. "What are you doing?" I asked, finally relenting and helping her get it off.

She lifted it off my palm and held it up. "There were so many things I couldn't say the night we got married, but want to say now."

I ran my hand down her cheek and wiped another tear that fell, but then just like that, the tears were gone and she picked up my hand.

"Growing up the way I did, I never imagined meeting anyone like you. In fact, I never let myself dream because dreams seemed like an excellent way to get your heart broken. Instead, I did the sensible things, I loved the sensible people, and I learned pretty quickly that rational and sensible was boring. Sensible can be dangerous, and rational is fearful. Then I met you, and I started to dream. The dreams didn't feel boring the way sensible did. They were exciting and a never-ending series of *what-ifs* that I would never tire of. Every time I dreamed about being your wife on more than just paper, I knew I was asking for a broken heart, but I kept dreaming. You made me feel safe when you held me every night, and I needed that. I was afraid that like my dreams, this would end, too. You would leave me and I would be alone and scared again. In the month we've been married, you've already shown me everything you vowed a minute ago. You've been by my side in sickness and been an excellent nurse in getting me back to health. You've kept me safe and loved me unconditionally, even when I couldn't accept myself. With this ring, I give you my heart, my soul, and my body." She slipped the ring back on my finger and I gathered her into my arms.

"Mr. Kiss, you may kiss your bride," I said in a goofy pastor voice and she laughed for just a moment until my mouth smothered the sound from her lips.

The kiss started out tender and gentle, but quickly spiraled into a passion I couldn't, and didn't want to, control. Her whimper finally broke through the need in my brain. "I'm sorry, did I hurt you?" I asked, my hand going to her cheek.

"You'll never hurt me. Please, make me your wife," she begged, clinging to my shirt.

I picked her up and carried her to our room, where the bedside lamp burned. There were pink rose petals all over the bed and I lifted a brow. "Very nice touch." I grinned, bending down to nuzzle her neck.

She sighed when I laid her on the bed and she wound her hands in my hair, trapping me there. "Don't you want to see what's under the robe, Mr. Kiss?" she asked seductively.

I laid my hand over her chest and stole another kiss. "I already know." She raised a brow and I leaned in close to her ear, "my heart."

About The Author

Katie Mettner

Katie Mettner writes small-town romantic tales filled with epic love stories and happily-ever-afters. She proudly wears the title of, 'the only person to lose her leg after falling down the bunny hill,' and loves decorating her prosthetic leg with the latest fashion trends. She lives in Northern Wisconsin with her own happily-ever-after and three mini-mes. Katie has a massive addiction to coffee and Twitter, and a lessening aversion to Pinterest — now that she's quit trying to make the things she pins.

The Snowberry Series

Snow Daze

Trapped in an elevator with a handsome stranger was the perfect meet-cute, but Dr. Snow Daze wasn't interested in being the heroine of any romance novel. A serious researcher at Providence Hospital in Snowberry, Minnesota, Snow doesn't have time for a personal life, which was exactly the way she liked it.

Dully Alexander hated elevators, until he was stuck in one with a beautiful snow angel. Intrigued by her gorgeous white hair, and her figure-hugging wheelchair, he knows he'll do anything to be her hero.

When a good old-fashioned Minnesota blizzard traps them at her apartment, he takes advantage of the crackling fire, whispered secrets on the couch, and stolen kisses in the night. Dully will stop at nothing to convince Snow she deserves her own happily ever after.

December Kiss

It's nearly Christmas in Snowberry Minnesota, but Jay Alexander is feeling anything but jolly. Stuck in the middle of town square with a flat tire on his worn-out wheelchair leaves him feeling grinchy.

December Kiss has only been in Snowberry for a few months when she happens upon this broken-down boy next door. His sandy brown hair and quirky smile has her hoisting his wheelchair into the back of her four horse Cherokee.

When a December romance blooms, Jay wants to give December just one thing for Christmas, her brother. Will Jay get his December Kiss under the mistletoe Christmas Eve?

Noel's Hart

Noel Kiss is a successful businessman, but adrift in his personal life. After he reconnects with his twin sister, Noel realizes he's bored, lonely, and searching for a change. That change might be waiting for him in Snowberry, Minnesota.

Savannah Hart is known in Snowberry as 'the smile maker' in Snowberry, Minnesota. She has poured blood, sweat, and tears into her flower emporium and loves spreading cheer throughout the community. She uses those colorful petals to hide her secrets from the people of Snowberry, but there's one man who can see right through them.

On December twenty-fourth, life changes for both Noel and Savannah. He finds a reason for change, and she finds the answer to a prayer. Desperate for relief, Savannah accepts Noel's crazy proposal, telling herself it will be easy to say goodbye when the time comes, but she's fooling no one.

Noel has until Valentine's Day to convince Savannah his arms are the shelter she's been yearning for. If he can't, the only thing he'll be holding on February 14th is a broken heart.

April Melody

April Melody loved her job as bookkeeper and hostess of Kiss's Café in Snowberry, Minnesota. What she didn't love was having to hide who she was on the inside, because of what people saw on the outside. April may not be able to hear them, but she could read the lies on their lips.

Martin Crow owns Crow's Hair and Nails, an upscale salon in the middle of bustling Snowberry. Crow hid from the world in the tiny town, and focused on helping women find their inner goddess. What he wasn't expecting to find was one of Snowberry's goddesses standing outside his apartment door.

Drawn together by their love of music, April and Crow discover guilt and hatred will steal their future. Together they learn to let love and forgiveness be the melody and harmony in their hearts.

Liberty Belle

Main Street is bustling in Snowberry, Minnesota, and nobody knows that better than the owner of the iconic bakery, the Liberty Belle. Handed the key to her namesake at barely twenty-one, Liberty has worked day and night to keep her parents' legacy alive. Now, three years later, she's a hotter mess than the batch of pies baking in her industrial-sized oven.

Photographer Bram Alexander has had his viewfinder focused on the heart of one woman since returning to Snowberry. For the last three years she's kept him at arm's length, but all bets are off when he finds her injured and alone on the bakery floor.

Liberty found falling in love with Bram easy, but convincing her tattered heart to trust him was much harder. Armed with small town determination and a heart of gold, Bram shows Liberty frame-by-frame how learning to trust him is as easy as pie.

Wicked Winifred

Winifred Papadopoulos, Freddie to her few friends, has a reputation in Snowberry, Minnesota. Behind her back, and occasionally to her face, she's known as Wicked Winifred. Freddie uses her sharp tongue as a defense mechanism to keep people at bay. The truth is, her heart was broken beyond repair at sixteen, and she doesn't intend to get close to anyone ever again. She didn't foresee a two-minute conversation at speed dating as the catalyst to turn her life upside down.

Flynn Steele didn't like dating. He liked speed dating even less. When his business partner insisted, he reluctantly agreed, sure it would be a waste of time, until he met the Wicked Witch of the West. He might not like dating, but the woman behind the green makeup intrigued him.

A downed power pole sets off a series of events neither Flynn nor Winifred saw coming. Their masks off, and their hearts open, they have until Halloween to decide if the scars of the past will bring them together or tear them apart. Grab your broomstick and hang on tight. This is going to be a bumpy ride...

Nick S. Klaus

Nick S. Klaus is a patient man, but living next door to Mandy Alexander for five years has him running low this Christmas season. He wants nothing more than to make her his Mrs. Klaus, but she'd rather pretend he isn't real.

Mandy Alexander is a single mom and full-time teacher. She doesn't have time to date or for the entanglements it can cause. Even if she did have time, getting involved with her next-door neighbor, and co-worker, Nick S. Klaus, had disaster written all over it.

This Christmas, Nick's determined to teach Mandy that love doesn't have to be complicated, and he's got two of the cutest Christmas elves to help him get the job done. Will this be the year Santa finally gets his Mrs. Klaus under the mistletoe?

A Note to My Readers

People with disabilities are just that—people. We are not 'differently abled' because of our disability. We all have different abilities and interests, and the fact that we may or may not have a physical or intellectual disability doesn't change that. The disabled community may have different needs, but we are productive members of society who also happen to be husbands, wives, moms, dads, sons, daughters, sisters, brothers, friends, and co-workers. People with disabilities are often disrespected and portrayed two different ways; as helpless or as heroically inspirational for doing simple, basic activities.

As a disabled author who writes disabled characters, my focus is to help people without disabilities understand the real-life disability issues we face like discrimination, limited accessibility, housing, employment opportunities, and lack of people first language. I want to change the way others see our community by writing strong characters who go after their dreams, and find their true love, without shying away from what it is like to be a person with a disability. Another way I can educate people without disabilities is to help them understand our terminology. We, as the disabled community, have worked to establish what we call People First Language. This isn't a case of being politically correct. Rather, it is a way to acknowledge and communicate with a person with a disability in a respectful way by eliminating generalizations, assumptions, and stereotypes.

As a person with disabilities, I appreciate when readers take the time to ask me what my preferred language is. Since so many have asked, I thought I would include a small sample of the people-first language we use in the disabled community. This language also applies when leaving reviews and talking about books that feature characters with disabilities. The most important thing to remember when you're talking to people with disabilities is that we are people first! If you ask us what our preferred terminology is regarding our disability, we will not only tell you, but be glad you asked! If you would like more information about people first language, you will find a disability resource guide on my website.

Instead of: He is handicapped.
Use: He is a person with a disability.

Instead of: She is differently abled.
Use: She is a person with a disability.

Instead of: He is mentally retarded.
Use: He has a developmental or intellectual disability.

Instead of: She is wheelchair-bound.
Use: She uses a wheelchair.

Instead of: He is a cripple.
Use: He has a physical disability.

Instead of: She is a midget or dwarf.
Use: She is a person of short stature or a little person.

Instead of: He is deaf and mute.
Use: He is deaf or he has a hearing disability.

Instead of: She is a normal or healthy person.
Use: She is a person without a disability.

Instead of: That is handicapped parking.
Use: That is accessible parking.

Instead of: He has overcome his disability.
Use: He is successful and productive.

Instead of: She is suffering from vision loss.
Use: She is a person who is blind or visually disabled.

Instead of: He is brain damaged.
Use: He is a person with a traumatic brain injury.

Other Books by Katie Mettner

The Fluffy Cupcake Series (2)

The Kontakt Series (2)

The Sugar Series (5)

The Northern Lights Series (4)

The Snowberry Series (7)

The Kupid's Cove Series (4)

The Magnificent Series (2)

The Bells Pass Series (5)

The Dalton Sibling Series (3)

The Raven Ranch Series (2)

The Butterfly Junction Series (2)

A Christmas at Gingerbread Falls

Someone in the Water (Paranormal)

White Sheets & Rosy Cheeks (Paranormal)

The Secrets Between Us

After Summer Ends (Lesbian Romance)

Finding Susan (Lesbian Romance)

Torched

Made in the USA
Middletown, DE
23 December 2022